DEMONS
IN THE
ROUGH
THE REALM SERIES

AE JONES

AE Jones: Demons in the Rough

Copyright © 2021 by Amy E Jones

Publisher: Gabby Reads Publishing LLC

Cover Designer: theillustratedauthor.net

Editor: demonfordetails.com

PRINT

ISBN: 978-1-941871-33-1

AUTHOR'S NOTE

When I started writing the Realm books, I quickly realized that some of the scenes would need to crossover into the other books. Misha, Aleksei and Sergei's stories are interlocking in time—it's a close family, after all—so as you're reading the first three books, you'll probably notice some scenes you've read before...but from a very different perspective. Amazing what you can learn from a new point of view.

I originally planned on only writing a trilogy, but I couldn't get this family out of my mind. So two more books were born! Marrick first appears as Naya's loyal best friend in *Demons Are A Girl's Best Friend* and I wanted to tell this honorable demon's story.

And Boris...this over-the-top father and clan leader has a special place in my heart. How could I not give him a happy ever after?

Prepare for some fun with this outrageous but loving family!

Bobbi –
The realm series was supposed to be a trilogy about brothers finding their happy endings. But you kept telling me (over and over again) that you wanted to read more about this over-the-top demon family, and I realized that I wanted to write more about them too. So this book is for you.
Who says perseverance (pestering) doesn't pay off eventually?

CHAPTER 1

Marrick was a demon without a heart. Not a full one, anyway.

Sure, the actual muscle beat in his chest to feed his body with blood and air, but not with what he really needed—love and belonging.

And since he was the leader of the demon portal guard, it was not something he would be voicing out loud.

Plus as an empath, he was constantly bombarded by the emotions of others, which was why he kept his thoughts and feelings locked away. He couldn't possibly deal with his own needs when he was battered by the overwhelming emotions of others.

Until recently he hadn't thought he could have more in his life. Then his best friend and fellow guard, Naya, found her mate and moved to earth. Now she had a beautiful daughter named Kara.

And when he sensed how happy she was, he dared to wonder...what if?

But that was a dangerous, dangerous thought. He had a job to do.

He'd decided to follow in the footsteps of his parents and grandparents before him and volunteered to guard the five demon factions who were banned from earth. Now, more than a millennium later, the descendants of those factions were getting a second chance.

Fates, they were all getting a second chance. Everything was changing, and yet Marrick still stood guard over this valley that never changed.

Although the same couldn't be said of its inhabitants. The realm demons had spent centuries living in despair and hopelessness. Even the portal guards were trapped.

And being seen as the enemy, the jailer, takes a toll on anyone—especially someone who could sense others' emotions. Marrick hadn't realized how much until he began to help the realm demons.

Now those very demons could choose to migrate to earth. But since there were literally thousands of demons, it was not an easy task.

He would continue to guard—no, *watch over*—this world until all the demons who wanted to go to earth had left. And then he would finally leave as well.

The thought set the heart in question to pounding under his uniform's armor plating. What would it be like to live on earth? He traveled back and forth to help with the daunting process of relocating demons, but he still hadn't truly experienced what earth had to offer.

Even though Naya had left the guard, she still played a part in bringing the demons to earth, and helping her mate, Aleksei, with the leadership of the immigration bureau.

As if she sensed his thoughts—and since Naya was telepathic, maybe she did—the crystal he wore around his neck heated up, signaling that Naya was reaching out to him.

Yes, Naya?

How are you today, my friend?

Good. How is Kara?

She's wonderful. Naya huffed. *I'm good, too. Thanks for asking.*

Marrick smiled. *I was getting to you next.*

Get that wicked grin off your face.

She was telepathic, but even this was a stretch for her. *How?*

I don't need to see your face to know what you're doing. We've known each other our whole lives. Aleksei wants to know if you're coming to the immigration meeting later.

Yes, ma'am, he thought, with just the hint of sarcasm. *Tell your bossy mate I'll be there.*

Naya chuckled in his mind. *Smart-ass. See you soon.*

Marrick laughed to himself as he walked back toward the forest. Who would ever have thought he would find himself attending meetings and planning sessions?

He hadn't even known what a planning session was until Aleksei came to the realm and convinced the demons to work with the earthers and not against them. Not an easy feat, given the demons' animosity after centuries of being locked away. Most of the realm demons hadn't even been born when their clans were exiled.

Now they weren't prisoners any longer. If they wanted—and that was the important word, *if* they wanted—they could go to earth.

Maybe that was the biggest gift of all. After a millennium, the realm demons were allowed to choose their future. Which meant eventually so would he.

And could he dare hope someday it would lead to his heart being nourished by much more than blood and air?

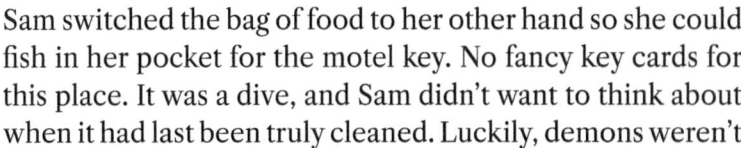

Sam switched the bag of food to her other hand so she could fish in her pocket for the motel key. No fancy key cards for this place. It was a dive, and Sam didn't want to think about when it had last been truly cleaned. Luckily, demons weren't as susceptible to germs as humans. Which was a good thing, considering the many tacky, run-down places she and her mother had stayed in over the years.

For the past few weeks she'd been working at a sandwich shop. They paid her less than minimum wage, but since they also paid her under the table, she had no one to complain to. And the fewer paper trails Sam and her mom left, the better for both of them.

The bonus was the shop manager let her have one free sandwich for lunch and for dinner. Naturally Sam had started skipping lunch so she could take two subs home.

She opened the door to find her mom sitting on a plastic circa-1970s chair next to the small desk they used as a table.

"Hey, Mom." She held up the bag.

Her mom pretended to think hard. "Let me guess, sandwiches?"

Sam's heart squeezed. Her mom didn't joke very often.

Sam set the bag down and plopped on the bed. "I mixed it up tonight. There was some leftover soup they let me have."

"Be still, my beating heart."

Sam laughed and sat up from her slouch. "I'll go wash up."

Coming back into the front room, she tensed when she noticed her duffel bag was packed and sitting on the other chair in the corner. They hadn't been in this latest town for even a month.

"Are we moving again?"

Her mom didn't answer, instead busying herself by pulling the sandwiches and soup out of the bag. Sam's nerves went into hyperdrive.

If they'd been discovered, her mother wouldn't be sitting and calmly unwrapping the sub sandwich. They'd already be on the road.

"What's going on?"

"Sit down and eat while the soup's still warm."

Sam sat down across from her but didn't touch her food.

Her mom sighed. "It's time for us to split up for a while."

Sam's stomach took a dive. "Why?"

"We've done this before."

Yes, and Sam despised it. She worried about her mother's safety every moment of every day she wasn't with her. "It doesn't mean we should do it again."

"It's time. We almost got caught two months ago, and I should have insisted we split up then. You know it's safer if we aren't together. It's much easier to move under the radar that way."

"Since when has the great Gwendolyn ever taken the easy way out?"

"Don't play to my ego, Samantha Taylor."

"Don't use my full first name and fake last name in that motherly tone."

He mother sighed. "There's nothing else to talk about. I found you a place to go."

Sam shook her head.

"It's perfect. It's a demon compound looking for a nurse."

"We don't even know if they'll take me. I don't have a degree."

"A human nursing degree. You've worked in demon clinics before, so you have plenty of experience. Don't you want to work in a demon hospital?"

Of course she did, but not if it meant losing her mother.

"You can come with me."

Her mother's eyes took on that familiar stubborn glint. "You know we can't be together in a demon compound. It's too risky, since I'm the one they're looking for. I won't let you be hurt."

Sam stood up and started pacing.

"Spit it out, Sam."

"This isn't a good idea."

"It's a great idea. I sent them your resumé and answered some online questions."

Sam spun and faced her. "You pretended to be me?"

"Of course. I'd do anything for you. There's a ticket sitting on top of your duffel for the bus leaving tonight."

"I am a hundred and fifty-seven years old, Mom. Why do you think you can still make decisions for me?"

"Because I'm your mother, and your safety and happiness mean everything to me. And I'm so sorry." Gwen waved her hands around. "This is not happiness. I've sucked you into this world, and it's time for you to break free."

"Don't. You have nothing to be sorry for."

"I should have protected you—us—better."

Sam sat across from her mom and grabbed her hand. "You're the best mom in the whole wide world." Her throat ached with memories when she repeated the expression she'd used as a child.

"And you're the best daughter in the whole wide world." Gwen swallowed. "We follow basic protocol. Burner phones and our scheduled contact times."

"I'm not leaving you, damn it."

"Language."

"I'm one hundred and fifty-seven. If I have a 'damn it' in me, I'm going to say it."

Her mom shook her head with a smile. "You've never been shy."

"I take after my mother. Besides, shy is boring."

"So you keep saying. But you could use a little boring in your life. I communicated with an Irina Chesnokov. She's been setting up the candidates to come and interview with their doctor, and she assured me the compound is safe. You'll probably be bandaging knees and giving shots in no time."

"Mom."

Her mom squeezed her hand. "You're going. We need to be safe, and right now being apart makes the most sense."

Sam blinked back tears.

"I want you to have as boring a time as possible."

Sam sighed. "Where am I going?"

"An eastern suburb in Cleveland, Ohio."

"Well then, you'll probably get your wish. How much excitement could there be in Cleveland, Ohio?"

CHAPTER 2

Sam checked her watch again. Damn. She was behind schedule. She hiked her backpack up on her shoulders while she waited for her duffel bag beside the bus where she'd just spent twelve long hours.

According to her mother, Irina had insisted on sending someone to pick her up at the bus station. Which seemed a bit over-the-top to Sam, but since she didn't have to spend money for a ride, it worked for her.

Cleveland, Ohio. Who would have thought she'd end up here? Sam and her mother had lived all over the US, but the Midwest was a new experience for her. She hated that she wasn't with her mother. She'd spent a large part of her childhood separated from her for protection, and as an adult she continued to fight for them to be together. But her mother still insisted they split up periodically so they couldn't be traced.

The bus driver removed the last of the luggage, and the other passengers went on their way. As Sam turned with her duffel, she noticed a small woman walking toward her, followed by a very large male. His bulk made her think he was a demon, and when he got closer, she could sense she was right. The woman had dark black, chin-length hair with purple tips. She felt human.

"Samantha?" the woman asked.

"Yes, but I go by Sam."

"Irina sent us. I'm Kyle, and this is Misha."

"Nice to meet you. Sorry for not meeting you out front. I was waiting for my luggage."

Misha reached for her bag, and she backed up a step.

Kyle patted his arm. "He looks intimidating, but he's a teddy bear at heart."

Misha shrugged. "Sorry if I scared you. I should have asked if you want me to carry your bag before reaching for it."

They headed toward the parking lot after Sam reluctantly let Misha carry the duffel. She climbed into the back seat of the SUV while Misha took the driver's seat and Kyle the front passenger seat.

"Welcome to Cleveland," Kyle said. "Have you ever been here before?"

"No," Sam said.

"It's a great city. Amazing people and sights." Kyle started pointing out landmarks as they drove along the highway. The more Kyle told her about the city, the more surprised Sam was at what Cleveland had to offer. But she wasn't going to get too excited. She never stayed in one place for long.

After a lull in the conversation, Misha chimed in. "You're forgetting about the most important part, Kyle. The food."

"You never let me forget about the food. Misha has the metabolism of a family of four." Kyle turned toward her and winked. "He can eat most anyone under the table."

"We'll have to take you some places like Little Italy once you're settled in."

Why were they being so friendly? "I don't have the job yet."

Kyle shrugged. "Irina must have seen something she liked in your resumé and correspondence."

Except Sam hadn't been the one to correspond with Irina, her mother had.

"Our teammate Sabrina will interview you as well. She's the head doctor at the demon hospital in the compound."

"Teammate?" Sam asked.

"Yeah. We work for the Bureau of Supernatural Relations."

Sam controlled her breathing. She hoped she wasn't visibly reacting. Her mother had told her she had a tendency to let people know what she was feeling just by the expression on her face.

But she was in a car right now with the paranormal police—the very last place she wanted to be.

Stay calm. "And why would a doctor from the BSR be working at the hospital?"

"Because the Shamat clan heads up the realm immigration."

And the surprises kept coming. Sam and her mother really hadn't paid much attention to the migration since they were on the run and weren't linked to a clan. "So you're all a part of the immigration project?"

Kyle nodded. "Yes. We're a part of it."

"But you're human," Sam blurted and then wanted to kick herself.

Kyle smiled. "I'm half human and half Majock, actually. So I have a vested interest in seeing the five realm clans return to earth."

She was part realm demon?

"Kyle is the person who convinced the Demon Council to allow the realm demons to come to earth," Misha said.

Sam had heard that someone spoke out to the Council. "That was you?"

Kyle's face pinkened a little. "Yep. But it wasn't just me. We all worked on it together. I just was the spokesperson because I have the biggest mouth."

Misha chuckled. "So true, little one."

The SUV slowed as they pulled up to a gate. A large male emerged from a gatehouse and waved them through when he caught sight of Misha.

When they drove into the compound, Sam stared at the surroundings in shock. How rich was this clan? This wasn't a compound. This was a neighborhood with pretty, understated houses.

They pulled up in front of a one-story house with a covered walkway linking the house to a large building sitting next to it.

"This big building houses the community center and the demon immigration offices," Kyle said.

"And the house?"

"That's Irina's house. You'll be meeting with her first."

Sam nodded as she opened her car door.

"Let me grab your luggage," Misha said.

Misha carried her duffel to the front door, where a small woman with white, curly hair greeted them with a broad smile. She clapped her hands together. "Samantha. I'm so glad you made it! I'm Irina. Come in, come in."

"Hello, Irina. Please call me Sam. It's nice to meet you."

"Mikhail, please put the luggage in the spare bedroom with the two twin beds. She'll stay here a few days until we can get her apartment set up. Then you and Kyle need to hurry over to the community center or you're going to be late for the meeting."

Kyle nodded. "Yes, Irina. Good to see you too, Irina."

Irina laughed. "Don't give me any of your lip, Kyle. You know how Aleksei is. Get going."

The big demon Misha came out of the bedroom and kissed Irina on the forehead before heading outside.

"Nice to meet you," Kyle said with a short wave before she closed the door.

Sam's head was spinning and she'd only been in the house for two minutes. "I wasn't expecting to stay here. I can find a hotel."

Irina beckoned for her to follow. "No need. Come sit down. There is much to discuss."

"Do you mind if I use the restroom?"

"Oh, of course I don't mind. How silly of me not to ask. Your bedroom is down the hall, the second door to the right. There's a bathroom attached to it."

Sam went down the hall and into the room, where she looked around. The room had two twin beds, a tall dresser, and a closet. The walls were painted light blue and a flower comforter was neatly folded on each bed. On the wall hung a large corkboard in the shape of Spiderman, with crayon drawings of superheroes and stick-figure family pictures tacked on in no particular order.

Sam turned slowly to take in everything. Irina was not at all what she'd expected. Sam went into the bathroom and smiled at the Superman bath mat and towels.

When she returned to the front of the house, she found Irina sitting in a comfortable chair in the living room. Irina gestured for her to take a seat on the couch.

"Would you like some iced tea and brownies?"

Sam didn't have to be asked twice. She reached for a brownie and took a big bite.

Irina laughed. "I like your enthusiasm! Welcome to my home. I hope the bedroom will work for you."

"Absolutely. Thank you. I see there are some resident artists who visit you."

"My great-grandsons, Matty and Luke, like to spend time with me. It's their room when they stay overnight."

"I really don't want to put you out. I can stay in a hotel."

Irina waved her hand. "Nonsense. You can stay here for a couple of days. Then we'll get you settled in the small apartment complex on the other side of the community center. An apartment just came available and will be perfect for you."

"I still have to interview. I might not get the job."

"Pfffft. I have a good feeling about you. I think you'll do just fine with your interview tomorrow."

Sam's throat tightened. She wasn't used to people doing something nice for her. Was there a catch?

"I'm so glad you reached out to me and applied for a job."

Sam's mom had shared her correspondence back and forth with Irina so Sam wouldn't be taken by surprise about anything. And yet there'd already been a couple of big surprises.

"I didn't realize this hospital helps with the demon migration."

"Yes. Our clan has really been the one to lead the migration, so we're working on expanding our medical facilities to help with that. Sabrina will explain everything during your interview tomorrow."

Sam set the half-eaten brownie on a napkin when her stomach threatened to rebel. When was the last time she'd been on an actual interview for a job she cared about?

Irina reached over and patted her hand. "You'll do great tomorrow. Here's a thought. Would you like to explore the compound for a while? We can meet back here in a couple of hours and have lunch together, and I'll answer any questions you have. And besides, you probably want to stretch your legs after the long bus ride. Do you have any food allergies or things you don't like to eat?"

"I'll eat anything. Are you sure?"

"Absolutely."

"Then I would love to walk around."

And scope out her surroundings in case she needed to make a run for it. But that wasn't something she'd share with Irina.

A few minutes later Sam strolled alongside a scenic lake, shaking her head. This couldn't be real. Who lived like this, really? Could this be the break she and her mom had been waiting for? Sam wouldn't get her hopes up too soon. Even though Irina seemed like a good-hearted, genuine person, it could change in an instant. And she had no idea what the others who lived here would be like.

She looked at the large building in front of her and wondered what was inside. Would it hurt if she took a peek? It was called a *community* center, after all. And she was technically part of the community...unless she made a run for it again.

She hurried to the side door of the center before she could change her mind and opened the door. No alarms sounded, so she walked right in. *Go forward with confidence* had always been her motto.

She wandered down the hall and looked into the rooms. Some small conference rooms were first, and then a mammoth exercise space with equipment came next. Could everyone in the compound exercise there? She crossed the hall and found a large industrial kitchen too. This place was frou-frou for sure.

Sam heard voices and followed them down the hall, pausing before she reached the door and peeking into what turned out to be a large gathering space. There was a long table toward the front of the room where Kyle and Misha were sitting with three others. This must be the meeting Irina had mentioned earlier. Next to Misha sat a petite blond human, and next to Kyle was a striking demon female. At the end of the table sat a dark-haired male who checked his watch before sighing.

The dark-haired female sitting beside him rested her hand on his. "Take a breath."

The male held her hand for a moment before letting it go. "Have you spoken with Marrick?"

"Yes. He should be here soon."

"Even my father can't seem to be on time."

Kyle laughed. "I thought you would have learned how to chill out by now, Aleksei. Let's get started with the meeting, and they'll show up...or not."

The male—Aleksei—nodded before reaching for the tablet in front of him.

"Okay. In two weeks we have another group of demons arriving from the realm. A hundred of them."

Kyle let out a whoop. Sam bit her lip to keep from laughing out loud.

"Aleksei, your team is rockin' it," Kyle said.

Aleksei's eyebrow rose before his mouth quirked up. "I'm here to serve, Kyle."

Kyle laughed out loud. "Glad you finally realized it." She turned to the female sitting next to her. "Naya, I think we have you to thank for reforming him."

Naya opened her mouth and emitted a high-pitched squeal. *What in the world?*

Naya turned to look behind her. "It appears that Kara wants to be part of the meeting." She reached down and picked up a squirming baby, who looked just like her mother except for huge emerald-green eyes that dominated her face.

Aleksei's frown was replaced by a huge grin. "Did you have a nice nap, sweetie?"

Kara reached for him and squealed again.

"You're spoiling her," Naya said, but with a smile, as she handed the baby to Aleksei.

"She's my daughter. Of course I'm spoiling her." He bounced the baby in his lap. "Callie, why don't you continue with the update?"

The petite blond nodded before looking down at her laptop. "We have the halfway houses set up for the new-comers. We're also arranging for the mentors who will help transition the demons to earth."

"What about the physicals to see about health issues?" Kyle asked.

"Sabrina already sent a medical team through a week ago, and they checked everyone who's immigrating this time. Since we have already established the healers in the villages, they've helped speed things up," Callie said.

"Have we been getting any pushback from the Council?" Misha asked.

Aleksei sighed. "When don't we get pushback from the Demon Council? There will always be those who resist bringing the five clans to earth. We'll just keep moving ahead and prove them wrong."

Sam understood to a certain extent where the Coun-cil was coming from. Why would they bring such power-ful demons to earth? In her experience, they already had enough trouble with the higher-level demons on earth, so why add to the problem?

Chapter 3

Marrick wound through the trees as he headed farther into the forest. He didn't normally create a portal out in the open, and even though the realm had calmed down, he still didn't want to risk another demon coming through.

He concentrated, creating the portal that would take him to earth. The air in front of him shimmered while his skin and eyes changed to his human form before he stepped through. In the realm they remained in their demon form, but of course once they moved to earth that wouldn't work. So all the realm demons were busy learning to turn in preparation for living on earth one day.

He hadn't known what to expect the first time he turned. Naya's human form had brown skin and brown eyes, and many of the other realm demons' human forms were a variety of beige, tan, and brown. Definitely not the bright hues of their demon clan colors. It still shocked him when his skin lightened to a warm tan color after centuries of living with purple skin.

He entered the portal. By now he should be used to traveling this way, but it still felt like he was breathing underwater.

He emerged into the large room.

The group sitting around the table gaped at him for a moment before Kyle blurted, "Marrick?"

"Yes."

Her eyes got very big. "Wow, your human form is *fine*."

Misha laughed before shaking his head. "It's a good thing your mate isn't here right now, little one."

Kyle laughed. "Just cause I'm in love with Dalton doesn't mean I can't appreciate a good-looking male when I see him."

Heat rushed to Marrick's face. "I've been practicing changing to my human form."

"Good job," Kyle said.

Naya stood and gripped forearms with him in the usual realm greeting. "Good to see you, my friend."

He sat down in the empty chair next to her while Kara babbled at him before giggling. She recognized him even in human form.

Aleksei sighed. "Quit it, you little flirt."

Kara ignored her dad and held out her hands to Marrick, who stood, scooped her up, and kissed her on the cheek.

Kyle and Naya laughed. Kyle said, "You're in so much trouble, Aleksei."

Aleksei shook his head. "Marrick, let's hear your report on the realm."

"Overall things are calm. No skirmishes or protests about the migration."

"We just sent a new shipment of supplies," Aleksei said.

"Yes, Lela and Sergei are at the central supply building sorting the new supplies and working with the clans. They should be returning to earth in the next day or two, earth time."

"Great." Aleksei looked down at his tablet. "Is there anything else we need to be concerned about? Something else we should be working on for those demons still in the realm?"

Marrick looked down at the babe sitting in his lap. "We've been trying to get the clans to work together more, but they're still reluctant."

Naya nodded. "The clans have spent a millennium trying to survive, and it's hard for them to learn how to cooperate."

"But it's going to be inevitable once they come to earth," Aleksei said.

Marrick's empathic senses picked up emotion that wasn't coming from anyone at the table. Looking toward the doorway leading to the hall, he saw a flash of motion. Who was listening to their conversation? He didn't sense any malicious emotions emanating from whoever it was. It was more curiosity, but he would be cautious anyway.

He handed the baby to Naya so he was free to intervene if necessary. *Someone is watching us in the hall.*

Naya nodded and held her daughter a little tighter.

Before Marrick could stand, Boris burst into the room through a side door.

"Hello, all! Have I missed everything?"

"Nice of you to join us, Father," Aleksei said.

"Sorry I'm late. I just stopped at your grandmother's house. She apparently is letting some stranger stay with her."

"You met Sam," Kyle said.

"She wasn't at Irina's. She is wandering around the compound unaccompanied."

"Who's Sam?" Aleksei asked.

"She's interviewing for a nursing position," Boris said.

"We picked her up at the bus station. She seems nice," Misha said.

Boris frowned.

Marrick was trying to follow the conversation, but he felt a change from the person in the hallway. The curiosity he felt earlier was slowly changing to anger.

Misha's eyebrows went up. "Don't you think Babushka can take care of herself?"

Boris's eyes widened. "You don't think it's important to learn who is staying with your grandmother? Irina handled everything about this without consulting me. We don't know anything about this female."

Aleksei leaned on his elbows. "Babushka is tough and smart. She's not going to let anyone take advantage of her."

A burst of anger flowed to Marrick, and he stood as the source of the emotions appeared in the doorway.

"I'm not a criminal," she called out.

The female was petite, but she could still be a threat. Long brown hair hung to her shoulders, and fire seemed ready to burst from her green eyes.

Everyone at the table stood while Aleksei moved to stand in front of Naya and the baby.

Kyle and Misha didn't appear too concerned, but they did exchange a cryptic glance.

Boris stepped forward. "I'm sorry. Can I help you?"

The female frowned. "I'm not here to hurt anyone."

Boris's confusion showed, but he maintained his composure. "We haven't met. I'm Boris."

"Well, I'm Sam, the *female* staying with Irina."

Boris held up his hands. "I'm sorry. I meant no offense."

Kyle circled the table. "Boris can be heavy-handed when it comes to protecting his family, but everyone is treated with respect here."

Sam's chin hiked up. "I told Irina I could stay in a hotel, but she insisted I stay with her. But I can understand why you want to protect your mother. I'll move into a hotel tonight."

Boris took another step closer. "No. I apologize for assuming the worst and giving you the wrong first impression of our clan."

Sam stared back at him as silence reigned for a moment.

Kyle spoke first. "Now that awkwardness has descended upon us, let me introduce you to everyone else. You already know Misha. This is Callie. She's the right-hand woman of the demon immigration bureau and Misha's wife."

"Hi, Sam, welcome."

"And this is Aleksei. He's the head of the bureau. Naya was a realm guard who, for reasons that escape me, fell in love with Aleksei, and this is their wonderful daughter, Kara."

Aleksei chuckled. "You never cease to amaze me, little sister."

Kyle rolled her eyes. "That's my goal. And, last but not least, this is Marrick. He's a realm guard who helps us with the immigration."

Marrick nodded to her, and after a second Sam looked down at the floor. She was losing her fire, and he sensed embarrassment settling in.

"I'll let you get back to your meeting."

Aleksei sighed. "I think we're done for tonight."

"Well, now that Marrick has mastered his human form, I want to show him around the compound," Naya said.

Marrick's heart sped up. He had never really seen the compound before.

"Of course." Aleksei held out his hands to the baby, and she reached for him with a squeal. "Sam, if you'd like to go with them, Naya can show you around as well."

"I don't know."

"I'll tag along too," Kyle said. "We'll show you all the hot spots."

Misha laughed before grabbing the laptop with one hand and Callie's hand with the other. "Not sure what your definition of hot spot is, Kyle."

"Come on, Sam," Kyle said.

"Okay."

Kyle gestured for them to head out the door, and Marrick and Naya fell in step behind them.

Once outside, Marrick took in a deep breath of clean air. In the realm, the air always felt dusty. He jerked to a stop and looked around, trying to keep his mouth from hanging open as he took everything in. Or tried to.

Naya slapped him on the shoulder. "It's amazing, isn't it?"

"I don't know what to say."

Sam and Kyle had walked a few steps but paused when they realized he and Naya weren't following them.

"Is everything okay?" Sam asked.

Marrick wasn't exaggerating when he said that he was speechless, so it was good that Kyle spoke for him. "Marrick has never been outside the community center before. He's seeing our world for the first time."

He cleared his throat. "I went to the healing center with Naya when she was sick, but nowhere else."

Sam's eyes widened. "Wow. Your world isn't like this?"

"No. We live in small huts and grow and hunt for our food." He looked around. "I have seen pictures of earth."

"But it sure isn't the same as seeing it live," Sam said.

A strange noise to his right had him reaching for the knife in his belt.

Naya placed a hand on his arm. "It's okay. It's a car."

He watched as a large box with a male inside rolled down the street. "Is it a weapon?"

"It's used for transportation, a motorized cart."

They continued down the hard path. Houses sat on each side of the wider path where the cars traveled. But they weren't like any houses he'd ever seen. Kyle pointed out different buildings to Sam, but Marrick didn't understand much of what they were talking about.

They stopped in front of the large building where the sick were tended to and where Naya had been.

"This is the hospital," Kyle said.

"My interview is here tomorrow," Sam said.

"Are you a healer?" Marrick asked.

Sam nodded. "I'm a nurse."

"Healers are special," he said.

Sam looked away. Why she was embarrassed, he had no idea, but it was coming through loud and clear.

They went down another street—at least that's what Naya called it, a "street"—and came to a house with a small, furry beast making strange noises at a tree.

"That's a dog," Naya said. "And you won't understand what it's saying. It's called barking, and we can't interpret it."

"Why is it talking to a tree?" Marrick said.

Kyle looked up into the branches. "Misha! What are you doing up there?"

Marrick glanced at Sam, who looked as confused as he felt. Then he turned to Naya. "Where is Misha?" he whispered.

Naya pointed. "Kyle isn't seeing things. Misha is sitting on that branch."

Marrick looked up to where Naya was pointing. Another furry beast sat in the tree. "Can Misha turn into a beast?"

Naya smiled and shook her head. "No. That beast, as you call him, belongs to the twins, and it's a cat. A big cat."

Kyle laughed. "It's huge, which is why the boys named him after their father. Misha likes to eat. Don't you, boy?"

Meow.

The front door of the house opened and a female came out. "Bruno! Leave that cat alone. Come on, boy." The dog ran to her and she waved to them. "Sorry about that."

Naya waved back. "Don't worry, Susan, it's okay."

Kyle held up her hands. "Come on, Misha. It's time to go home. The twins are going to be worried about you."

The cat appeared to ignore her. Was it hard of hearing?

"Can I help?" Marrick volunteered.

"You can try," Kyle said. "But be careful, he has claws."

"Hello, cat," he said loudly. "I'm going to pick you up now and take you to your home." Marrick reached up and wrapped his hands around the cat's middle.

A strange noise erupted from the cat before it felt like a handful of thorns lodged in his hand.

"Oh, be careful," Sam said.

Marrick picked up the cat and brought it down to his chest. The cat blinked up at him.

"Misha and Callie's house is down the street. Do you think you can hold onto him until then?" Kyle asked.

Marrick nodded and they walked a few houses down until Kyle jogged up to a door and knocked.

Misha—the demon, not the cat—opened the door. The cat squirmed in Marrick's arms and, with a pitiful howl, launched himself into the air and ran inside.

"Thanks for bringing him home. The boys have been looking all over for him."

"A dog had him up a tree, and Marrick saved him," Kyle said.

"Did he draw blood?" Misha asked.

Marrick looked down at his hand. "Just a little."

"Here, let me see," Sam said and took his hand.

"Your blood's green," she said with wide eyes.

"Yes, in the realm it's green," Naya said. "If he ever stays here for a longer period of time, it would turn red."

"Do you have a first-aid kit?" Sam asked.

"Yes," Misha said before beckoning them inside the house.

Now it was Marrik's turn to be embarrassed. "This is nothing. I'm fine."

She shook her head. "I know it'll heal quickly, but we should still disinfect it before you head back to the realm."

When they entered the house, it was Marrick's turn to gape again. What were all these things in the house?

Naya laughed before slapping him on the back. "It's a lot to take in. I wasn't going to show you the inside of a house until the next time you came to earth. Sorry."

Two identical little boys barreled into the room and hollered when they saw the cat sitting on the floor.

"Misha! Where have you been?"

Meow.

The demon Misha walked into the room carrying a box and handed it to Sam. "Boys, Marrick rescued your cat. You should thank him."

The boys trooped over to Marrick and grinned up at him. "You look good as a human," the twin to the right said.

He cleared his throat. "Thank you."

"Do you remember us?" the twin to the left asked. "I'm Matty, and this is Luke."

Marrick narrowed his eyes at them as he sensed mischief flowing between them. "I think *you* are Luke, and *this* is Matty."

"How did you know?" they both asked at the same time.

"Boys!" Misha the demon said.

"Thank you for bringing Misha home. He tries to escape the house all the time," Matty said.

"Maybe you should call him Houdini," Kyle said. When the twins looked at her with puzzled frowns, probably similar to how Marrick imagined his face looked, Kyle continued. "Houdini was a human magician, an escape artist. Although now I think about it, maybe he was supernatural, which would explain how he did the things he did."

"Maybe you should call him anything else," Misha muttered.

"Papa," the twins said while shaking their heads in an identical gesture.

Misha sighed. "This is Sam. She just moved to the compound."

"Hi, Sam."

"Hello. I think I've already seen some of your artwork at Irina's house."

The boys bounced. "You know BB?"

She looked up, and Misha explained. "It stands for 'Babushka,' which means 'grandmother' in Russian."

"Yes. I met Irina today. She's a very nice lady. I'm staying in your bedroom at her house for a few days until I can get an apartment. I hope that's okay?"

Both twins nodded and then darted down the hall after Misha the cat.

Sam opened the box and pulled out a square of white. She ripped the edge and pulled out a smaller square, which had a strong smell.

"This is an alcohol swab," she explained to Marrick. "It'll clean the wound so it doesn't get infected, and it might sting a little. Let me see your hand."

Marrick held it out to her, and she rubbed the square lightly over the top of his hand. There was a slight twinge for a moment, followed by a cooling sensation.

She looked up at him. "I think you'll live." She winked at him.

"Were you worried I wouldn't? Are cats poisonous?"

Her eyes widened. "No. I'm sorry if I alarmed you."

He winked back at her.

She laughed. "Wow, I really fell for that one, didn't I?"

He shrugged. "Maybe."

She smiled back and then seemed to realize she was still holding his hand. She let go and they turned to the others...who were all staring at them with a variety of expressions. He didn't need to read their emotions to know Kyle and Naya were plotting something.

He cleared his throat. "Thank you. It's time for me to head back to the realm. I should go to the community center."

"You can leave from here if you want," Misha said.

"Are you sure?"

"Yes. Just let me tell the twins to stay in their bedroom first, or they'll want to tag along with you."

He stepped out of the room and Marrick and Naya grasped forearms.

"See you soon, my friend." Naya said.

"And you. Good to see you again, Kyle." He turned to Sam. "It was very nice to meet you, Sam."

"You too."

Misha returned and nodded.

Marrick activated the portal and shifted into his demon form just as he entered the light. Right before he was sucked inside, he felt a surge of emotions burst from Sam.

He looked back to see if something had happened and realized the emotions were directed at him.

And then he was in the void and landed in the in-between where the portal guards lived. The portal closed, and he thought about reactivating it again to head back to earth. To find out what had changed.

Why had Sam suddenly been scared of him?

CHAPTER 4

Sam took a deep breath before opening Irina's back door that led into her kitchen. Irina stood at the stove, stirring something.

"Perfect timing. I'm just finishing up lunch. You must be hungry. Did you have fun walking around the compound?"

"Yes. You have a beautiful place."

Irina smiled. "We're very proud of it. Did you meet anyone?"

Sam hesitated. "I met some people in the community center."

Irina turned and looked at her. "What aren't you telling me?"

Sam gaped at her.

"No, I'm not psychic. But I raised a son and grandsons, and they couldn't keep anything from me either, so spill."

Sam cringed slightly. "I kind of burst into a meeting."

Irina's eyes widened. "Why?"

"Because I heard one of them talking and wanted to tell him I'm not going to hurt you or take advantage of you."

Irina crossed her arms. "I can guess who that was."

"Boris was worried about you."

She shook her head. "Look at you, defending him. I can take care of myself."

Irina sounded just like her own mother, which had Sam blinking to keep the tears at bay.

Irina gestured for Sam to take a seat at the table before turning back to the stove and putting something on a plate.

"I went with grilled cheese and tomato soup. Not very creative."

"Sounds perfect to me," Sam said.

Irina set the plates on the table and followed up with the bowls of soup.

"Tell me who else you met at the center."

"I saw Kyle and Misha, which is why I stopped outside the meeting." She looked over at Irina. "Boris, of course. I also met Aleksei, Naya, and their baby. And Misha's wife, Callie. Misha and Aleksei are your grandsons?"

"Two of them. You haven't met Sergei, who's the youngest. He and his mate, Lela, are in the realm right now."

Sam nodded. "They were talking about them during the meeting. I also met Marrick after he came through the portal."

"That was amazing to see, wasn't it?"

"I was speechless."

"And so, after you interrupted the meeting, what happened?"

"Kyle and Naya showed Marrick and me around the compound."

"He must have been in his human form. Well, good for him!" And then they dug into their food while Irina peppered Sam with questions, and she told her the story of saving a cat named Misha and meeting the twins.

Irina laughed through the entire tale, and Sam managed to smile, but it felt a bit forced.

"So, tell me about yourself, Sam."

Sam's nerves jumped at the question. Even though it was an innocent one, Sam had been trained her whole life not to share personal details. Ever. "There isn't much to tell."

"What about your family?"

"I don't have any." The bitterness of the lie stung her throat.

"I'm sorry, dear." Irina looked at her for an uncomfortable moment. "Did your clan help?"

Sam shook her head. "I don't have a clan. I'm Dalmot, so a lower-level clan. And I don't have any powers to speak of."

Irina reached across the table and grabbed her hand. "You have a clan now. If you decide to stay here."

How could anyone be so willing to let a stranger in?

"Tell me about your clan, Irina."

And she did, telling Sam more about her son and grandsons and their newly found mates, and about how everyone worked together to help bring the realm demons to earth, and about the challenges they had faced so far with the immigration.

"Irina, I have a question. Where do the portal guards come from?"

Irina nodded. "When the five clans were sent to the realm, volunteers from the remaining twelve clans on earth became portal guards. Many of today's portal guards are children, grandchildren, or great-grandchildren of the original volunteers. In some ways they have been trapped along with the five clans."

Sam changed the subject. After a couple more questions, Irina stood and picked up the empty plates.

"Let me help," Sam said.

"I'm fine. Besides, I have to leave for a meeting at the community center in a couple minutes. Why don't you go rest for a little bit? I have a sneaking suspicion you didn't sleep last night on the bus."

"Not really." Sam couldn't risk sleeping on a bus, not when she wasn't sure who else was riding with her.

"Take a nap. And feel free to make yourself at home. Do you need anything before I head out?"

"No, Irina. Thank you for welcoming me into your home." Sam went back in the bedroom, shut the door, and pulled out one of the burner phones.

She lay down on the bed and studied the crayon drawings on the wall until she heard Irina leave.

Then she sat up, dialed the number, and held her breath. She always did when she was waiting for her mom to answer the phone.

"Hello," the voice said in that familiar low tone. Her mom's voice felt like a warm blanket wrapping around her.

"Hi."

"Are you settling in?"

"Yes, it's very nice here. But this isn't exactly the laid-back location we thought it would be."

"What do you mean?" Her mom's voice tightened.

"This clan is part of the immigration efforts." Sam gave her a quick rundown of what she had learned so far, watching the clock on the nightstand. They normally kept their calls as brief as possible.

She told her about seeing the portal open and eavesdropping on the meeting. Her mom chuckled when Sam told her how she'd burst into the meeting.

"It's not funny. I should have minded my own business."

"It sounds like this Boris needed to be put in his place, and you spoke up for yourself. What was the realm demon like?"

Sam hesitated before speaking. "Okay."

"Okay? You saw him emerge from the portal and he was just okay? What aren't you telling me?"

Sam sighed. "When Marrick came through the portal, he was in his human form. He seemed nice, but then when he opened the portal to go back to the realm, he turned into his demon form. He's Pavel."

Gwen hesitated. "Just because he's Pavel doesn't mean he's bad."

"Sorry, but I'm not going to be so forgiving. Not after what they did to you, to our family. I don't trust them."

"I'm sorry, Sam."

"Why are you apologizing to me? *You* didn't do anything wrong."

"When is your interview?"

Her mother wasn't exactly subtle when she decided to change the subject. "Tomorrow."

"You'll be settled in there in no time."

"I don't even know if I have the job yet," Sam said.

"I have no doubt about that."

"You sound like Irina."

"I like her already and I haven't even met her."

Sam chuckled. "I think you two would get along great." Sam took a breath. "Are you okay?" She knew better than to ask where she was. Her mom wouldn't tell her, especially not over the phone.

"Of course I am. I'll talk to you soon. Love you."

"Love you too," Sam said as she ended the call. Even if her mother was facing down the devil himself, she would tell Sam she was okay.

Sam could only hope her mother was safe and staying out of trouble.

Gwen set her phone down and took a deep breath. So much had been running through her mind and her heart since she'd made the decision to send Sam away. Even though she hated pushing her daughter away, it was for the best. Especially if Sam could find a real clan to call her own.

It was time to stop running and face her demons—pun intended.

And she wanted Sam far away from her when it happened.

CHAPTER 5

Sam straightened her sleeve for the umpteenth time while she waited at the hospital front desk. After a few more sleeve tugs, she looked up to see a tall, beautiful female approaching her. She looked like a Swedish model. This was Dr. Miller?

"Sam?"

"Yes. Dr. Miller?"

"Yes, but please call me Sabrina." She gestured toward the hall, and they headed to her office.

Sabrina closed the door and sat down at a small round table after inviting Sam to take a seat as well.

"I understand from Irina, Misha, Kyle, and Boris that you're a nurse."

"Wow," Sam blurted.

"Yes, you have apparently made quite an impression. We're always looking for good nurses."

Sam cleared her throat. "Before we get started, I might as well tell you I don't have a nursing degree."

Sabrina smiled. "And you think that means the interview is over?"

"Maybe."

"I was practicing medicine before you could actually get a degree. So why don't you tell me about your experience?"

Sam took a breath and launched into her past nursing jobs. After a few minutes she realized she had been doing all the talking and Sabrina had said very little. Well, crap.

"I'm sorry. You should have interrupted me."

"Why? I can see how passionate you are about your job. Let me ask a couple of questions." And Sam answered them while Sabrina nodded. What did the nodding mean, exactly?

"What kind of questions do you have?" Sabrina asked.

"How does the hospital support the realm demons?"

"You know the Shamat clan runs the immigration?"

"Yes."

"At first we worked with the realm demons once they arrived here, giving physicals and helping with health issues. But we quickly discovered we needed to do more. So we actually have begun training healers in all the clan villages in the realm, and we provide medicines and other necessary supplies. So all the realm demons are getting healthy before they arrive, and the ones who decide to remain also receive health benefits."

"They want to stay there?"

"Some do. It's their home. And we're trying to make it better for those who remain."

"And the portal guards?"

"They'll get to decide if they want to remain in the realm or come to earth as well." Finally, Sabrina sat back. "I have one more question."

"Sure."

"When can you start?"

Sam blinked at her. "Seriously?"

"I wouldn't kid about something like this."

"I can start right now if you need me to."

Sabrina held up her hands. "I'll talk to Corinne, and she'll add you to the roster. Take a couple of days and get settled first. I understand you'll be moving into one of the apartments next to the community center."

Sam shook her head. "Everyone knows everyone else's business around here, don't they?"

Sabrina laughed. "Yep. You'll get used to it."

Sam wasn't too sure about that. She had learned to live under the radar, and so had her mother. Putting herself front and center might not be the best of ideas. But she wasn't going to think about it. She had a job!

She thanked Sabrina and left the hospital with a ridiculous grin on her face—even though she couldn't see it, she could tell by her cheek muscles that the smile was gigantic.

Sam walked the five minutes to Irina's house and hesitated for a moment before opening the door. Irina had insisted she was free to come and go, but it felt weird to just walk in.

She found Irina in the kitchen making lasagna. If Irina kept feeding her, she was going to gain serious weight.

"How did it go?" Irina asked.

"I got the job."

Irina pulled her into an awkward hug since her hands had cheese and marinara sauce on them.

"Of course you got the job," Irina said. "This calls for a celebration! What is your favorite dessert?"

"Anything you make," Sam answered quickly.

Irina tilted her head back and laughed. "You're wonderful. I think this celebration calls for more than dessert. Let's have a dinner party!"

"When?" Sam asked.

"Tonight, of course. I'm going to make some mac and cheese too, and we'll pack everything up and cook it in the community center kitchen."

"I'll help, but let me change out of my interview clothes first." Sam hurried down the hall into the bedroom and patted the superhero drawings hanging on the corkboard.

Maybe, just maybe, she was finally in a place where she could stay for a little while—a bit of a wild place for sure, but good, too.

Marrick stood outside the supply building watching the various realm demons talk to Sergei and Lela while they loaded supplies into handcarts.

The fact that Aleksei had agreed to bring supplies from earth to the realm had changed everything for the demons there. They had hope, which had been in short supply in the past. He felt a slight buzzing in his head.

Hello, Naya.

Marrick. How are things going?

Good. I'm with Sergei and Lela. We should be leaving shortly to head back to earth.

Great. Aleksei asked me to check to see how things are going, but don't tell Sergei.

Marrick chuckled inside his head. *What is it with those two stubborn males?*

They love each other to distraction. Aleksei can't help but look out for his baby brother.

Even though his baby brother is more than two hundred years old?

They're all a bunch of overprotective males. You've met Irina and Boris. It comes naturally to them.

Is Aleksei going to schedule another meeting since our last one ended abruptly?

Sam was an interesting interruption, wasn't she?

Yes.

Hmmm.

What did *hmmm* mean? But he wasn't going to ask.

After a moment Naya continued. *You seemed to like her.*

I didn't spend enough time with her to like her or not like her.

Hmmm.

He could sense just the hint of mischief. *What are you up to, my friend?*

Nothing. I just thought I saw something between the two of you. A spark.

He shook his head—and belatedly remembered she couldn't see him. *It doesn't matter if you sensed a spark. I sensed fear.*

Really? When? she asked.

Right before I went through the portal.

Naya paused before responding. *The idea of going to another world can be scary.*

Except he didn't think that was the problem. The fear had been directed at him. Why, he wasn't sure, but it had settled like a weight in his stomach.

Even though he'd only spent a short time with her, he wanted to understand why she was frightened. But what were the odds that he'd ever see her again? Unless she burst into another meeting.

"Marrick?"

He wished Naya goodbye and turned to Lela.

"Sorry. Did I interrupt something?"

"I was talking to Naya."

Sergei joined his mate and rested his arm across her shoulders. "Did Aleksei tell her to check up on us?"

Lela elbowed Sergei in the stomach. "Your brother loves you, and he's also in charge of all this."

"Are you two ready to head back to earth?" Marrick asked, hoping to change the subject.

"In a few minutes," Sergei said. "I want to review the inventory list one more time so I can make sure I have everything we need to bring next time."

"Thank you both for doing this. You've made a huge difference."

Lela shrugged. "Thank you. I couldn't not help the clans here. They're my blood too."

Marrick sent a telepathic message to Naya to let her know they would be arriving soon.

They went into the building and did a quick inventory check before heading into the forest to open a portal to earth.

Marrick turned into his human form. "Ready?"

Lela and Sergei nodded before the three of them stepped through the portal. Pressure surrounded him, but he didn't panic. Within seconds they arrived at the conference room at the community center.

Aleksei, Naya, and Kara greeted them, and Kara clapped her little hands and reached for Marrick.

Aleksei frowned. "I'm starting to get a complex."

Marrick grinned as he reached for Kara and threw her into the air before catching her. Kara giggled.

Aleksei turned to Sergei and Lela. "Glad you're home. How did things go?"

"Good. I'm surprised Grandmother isn't here," Sergei responded.

Naya smiled. "She's on her way. She insisted I call her when you got home."

Sergei laughed. "Why am I not surprised?" He held up a paper. "I have the list of needed supplies, which I'll coordinate with Callie tomorrow."

"Welcome home!" a voice called from the door, and they turned to watch Irina bustle toward them with Sam close behind. Why did he sense apprehension from Sam, especially when she looked at him?

"I know Sam has already met some of you. This is my grandson Sergei and his mate, Lela." Irina looked at Marrick. "Sam told me you had a run-in with the twins' ornery cat."

Why did Marrick constantly sense an aura of mischief surrounding Irina? And Sam was talking about him? "I'll survive."

"It's good to see you again, Sam," Aleksei said. "Sorry about last night. Hopefully you have forgiven Father for putting his foot in it."

Irina spoke up. "Sam has very kindly forgiven him. I, on the other hand, will be having a few words with my son. And you're more like your father than you want to admit, but I think Naya would step in if it began to show."

Naya laughed. "I would try, but the males in this family are a challenge."

"Yep," Lela said.

"Hey!" Sergei said before cuddling Lela closer. "You're supposed to stick up for me."

"Of course."

Marrick stopped himself from laughing. This family was a handful, and he was glad Naya had found her happiness with them. He looked over at Sam and caught her smiling at their antics, too and the sight made his heart kick up.

Then she glanced over at him and her expression froze. What had he done to her? Why did she react like that to him?

"Marrick?"

He turned to Irina.

"Congratulations on turning to your human form."

He nodded. "Yes, I thought it made sense to learn since I have to travel back and forth to earth."

"Well, I'd heard your human form was quite handsome. And I can see now that is the case."

Heat rushed to his face, and he looked over at Sam, who held up her hands.

"Don't look at me. I didn't say anything."

Irina looked between the two of them. "It was actually Kyle."

He bounced Kara, who squealed with delight. "I think it's time for me to head back to the realm." He handed Kara to Naya.

Irina rested her hand on his arm. "Don't be silly. We're just sitting down for dinner. You'll stay and celebrate with us."

He knew better than to fight this elder. She was a force to be reckoned with. "What are you celebrating?" he asked instead.

"Sam getting a new job at the hospital."

He nodded to Sam. "Congratulations."

She glanced down at the floor.

Before anyone could say anything else, the twins bounded into the room. "BB! What are we having for dinner?"

Callie came up behind the boys and placed her hands on their shoulders. "Matty, Luke. Say hi first. You don't start by asking about the food."

"Sorry," they both said at the same time.

Irina laughed. "That's okay, my rambunctious grandsons."

Misha joined them a few seconds later. "Babushka, I smell garlic. Please tell me we're having Italian for dinner."

The boys giggled.

"What did I miss?" Misha asked.

"Your sons are taking after you," Callie said.

Misha stood taller.

"Don't get too cocky, mister," Callie said.

The boys laughed even harder.

Irina clapped her hands. "Okay, the food is in the community kitchen. Everyone load your plates, and we'll eat in here at the conference room table."

Marrick followed the crowd into the room called a kitchen. His jaw dropped at all the things he saw. His hut had a fireplace and a shelf with pots and some clay plates. This room was magical or scary—or something he had no words for.

Naya stood next to him with Kara on her hip. "I'll explain what everything is. I had a hard time with some of the food at first, so I'll suggest some things for you."

He meant to pay close attention, but got distracted when Kara squealed at him.

Aleksei held out his hands. "Give me my daughter so she'll stop flirting with Marrick."

Marrick stifled a grin when Naya handed Kara to Aleksei and then handed him a plate. He spooned vegetables that she called a salad onto his plate, and also something called macaroni and cheese. He reached for the bread, but thought better of it when he caught the whiff of something strong-smelling coming from it.

"That's garlic bread. You might want to steer clear of it for now," Naya said.

Boris strode into the kitchen and opened his arms. "Hello, family! It's good to see you home, Lela and Sergei." He patted Marrick on the back. "Glad to see you're joining us too."

Everyone headed back to the conference room and sat down. Marrick took a bite of the food. The noodles—a strange name, but that is what Naya called them—had an interesting texture and the cheese sauce was quite flavorful.

"Do you like it?" one of the twins asked.

"Yes."

"BB makes Naya and us the mac and cheese whenever she makes lasagna for everybody else. We don't like all the stuff in the lasagna, and Naya doesn't like to eat meat," the other twin said.

"Thank you for sharing your food with me."

The boys proceeded to explain to him what all the vegetables were in the salad. He enjoyed the salad very much. It reminded him of some of the vegetables they grew in the realm.

"How was the trip?" Boris asked Sergei.

"Good. Lela got to spend some time with her father, and we made sure the supply chain we set up is working. I have a list of additional supplies we need to pull together."

"Excellent."

Marrick watched the family enjoy their meal and each other. It was refreshing to be with a group of people instead of eating his meals alone in his hut.

He looked across the table and saw Sam talking to Callie and Misha. He was glad she'd been accepted into this clan so easily.

When everyone finished their food, they took their plates into the kitchen and loaded them into a metal box that Naya explained would wash them. Irina then announced it was time to have something called a sundae for dessert.

"Can you only eat this on a Sunday?" Marrick asked.

The twins giggled. "It's not that kind of Sunday. It's an ice cream sundae."

The boys insisted on making the sundae for Marrick under the watchful eye of their mother.

Marrick took one bite of the cold mixture and what they called chocolate sauce and looked up at the boys, who were watching him expectantly.

"Well?" they both said.

"It's wonderful."

The boys smacked their hands together before sitting down at the table and enjoying their own sundaes.

Finally, everyone finished eating. Misha, Callie, and the boys left first, since the boys had schoolwork to complete. Boris kissed his mother on the head before he left as well, saying he had some Council work to complete.

"I should head back to the realm. Thank you for the dinner, Irina."

"Of course. It's good to have you spend time with us."

Lela and Sergei thanked him for bringing them back to earth, and Naya gripped his arm briefly before he backed away from them.

"Thanks, Marrick. We'll contact you when we're ready for another meeting," Aleksei said.

Marrick activated the portal and looked around for Sam, who stood over to the side. "It was good to see you again, Sam."

She nodded, and he wished he could ask what was troubling her.

He turned back into his demon form before entering the portal. He waited for the pressure, and it descended on him quickly, but he didn't emerge from the portal after a few seconds the way he normally did.

Instead, the air pushed against Marrick from all directions, threatening to crush him, and he tried not to panic.

But something was very wrong.

CHAPTER 6

Sam watched the portal in awe. She hadn't really gotten a good look at it the first time, and it was like watching a wall of opal fire. After a moment, flames pushed out like fingers.

"It should have closed by now. Something's wrong!" Naya said.

Aleksei ran over to the wall, slammed his hand against a panel, and an alarm sounded.

The flames in the portal started to shoot sparks.

"Everyone out! I'm going to lock down the room," Aleksei yelled.

"Lela!" Naya handed Kara off to Lela, who ran out of the room with the baby.

Naya and Aleksei stood in front of the portal, and Sergei joined them, gripping both their hands for a moment before dropping into a fighting stance. Apparently *they* weren't going anywhere.

Sam grabbed on to Irina and pulled her toward the door as well.

"I can stay and fight," Irina argued.

Before they could make it out of the room, a high-pitched whine pierced the space and the portal made a loud popping sound.

Sam looked back and saw Marrick fly out of the portal, through the air, and slam against the wall before crumpling to the ground.

She let go of Irina.

"What are you doing, Sam?" Irina asked.

"He's hurt. I can't just leave him there. Go on!"

Sam ran back and knelt next to Marrick and heard the click of locks in the door leading out of the room. She was in it for the long haul now.

Naya stood in front of the sputtering portal, guarding them from Fates only knew what. She yelled over her shoulder. "How is he?"

Sam placed her hand on his chest. His heart was pumping, and he was breathing, but taking only shallow breaths.

"He's alive."

She ran her hands over his arms and legs. They felt fine. But that didn't mean much unless they could x-ray him. Plus, she couldn't tell if he had any neck or back injuries. Even demons were susceptible to serious injuries they might not recover from.

"There's a first-aid kit in the cabinet," Aleksei said.

She ran to the cabinet and threw open doors until she found a box with a red cross on it and brought it with her to Marrick's side. Opening the box, she was surprised to find it wasn't a standard drugstore kit. This must be Sabrina's doing.

She pulled out a stethoscope and blood pressure cuff and listened to his heart and took his blood pressure.

She then pulled out several gauze pads and pressed them against the cut on his head. Head wounds bled a lot, and looked a lot worse than they were most times. Hopefully that was the case now.

When she pressed a little harder in an effort to stop the bleeding, he flinched.

She leaned down and spoke softly to him. "You're going to be okay."

Another high-pitched whine filled the room, and she threw herself on top of him to protect him from whatever was coming.

After a moment the whine stopped. She looked up to see the portal fizzle shut like the end of a fireworks show. Smoke circled where the opening had been.

Aleksei, Naya, and Sergei waited for another minute before they finally relaxed from their fighting stance.

As soon as Aleksei unlocked the doors, they slammed open to admit Boris, followed by Misha and several other very large demons.

Boris yelled over his shoulder to let medical in.

Sabrina came into the room with a couple of orderlies carrying equipment and a portable gurney.

"What do we have?"

"He shot out of the portal and slammed backward into the wall. Heartbeat is slow, but steady, and his breathing is shallow. BP is low—190 over 150. He's been unconscious, although he did respond to me putting pressure on the laceration on his temple. I don't know if he has a neck or back injury, so we should put a collar and backboard on just in case."

"Agreed."

Sabrina held her hands over his head and chest, as if sensing something, and then frowned.

"What is it?" Sam and Naya asked at the same time.

"His energy is all over the place. Let's get him to the hospital."

Sam pulled a collar out of the case the orderly had brought into the room and carefully secured it around his neck.

And when the orderlies placed him on a backboard, she secured the neck brace to it.

Naya looked from Marrick to Sam. "I have to stay and determine what happened in case we're under attack. Will you stay with him and let me know how he is?"

"Of course," Sam said, even though she was surprised Naya didn't ask Sabrina instead, since they knew each other. But she would see it through. He was her patient now.

They wheeled him slowly from the room.

"We have to be very careful transporting him. Even bumps over the sidewalk can be dangerous right now," Sabrina said.

Irina spoke up. "I can help with that." She turned her hands palm up and the gurney levitated a few inches above the ground.

Holy crap. Sam couldn't help gaping. Irina was one very powerful demon.

"Let's get him to the hospital," Irina said with a firm nod.

They walked through the building, and the orderlies opened the double doors so Irina could levitate Marrick outside. It didn't take them long to reach the hospital, and they moved Marrick into the triage room.

"We'll take it from here, Irina. Thank you," Sabrina said.

Irina backed into the hall.

Sabrina looked at Sam. "Guess you got put on the schedule sooner than you thought."

"That's okay. I want to see this through."

Sabrina nodded before she turned to her patient and the room filled with hospital personnel. "Okay, people. Sam's going to tell you what we know so far."

Sam gave a recap, and Sabrina ordered a series of tests while the rest of the staff hooked Marrick up to monitors.

"Once we know whether he has a neck or back injury, we'll remove his uniform, but not until then."

Sam looked down at the male in front of her. His skin was a pale violet color instead of the vibrant purple he'd been earlier. Green blood stained the side of his face.

She removed the soaked gauze. The cut looked superficial. She would still have recommended a CT, but Sabrina had already called for one.

And they got to work, Sam feeling right at home.

Russian curses blasted Boris's head. At least he had enough control not to say them out loud. He took a deep breath. He'd thought they finally moved beyond the constant opposition. But this felt like some sort of attack. It was too much of a coincidence that they were scheduled to bring the thousandth realm demon to earth in less than two weeks.

He couldn't think about what might have happened tonight if the portal somehow exploded. His family had been in that room. His beautiful granddaughter! More curses threatened to erupt.

Enough! It was time to figure out how to fix this, not dwell on what might have happened.

With the exception of security and hospital personnel, the rest of his clan was in the bunkers spaced throughout the compound for use in the event of an emergency.

Boris stood in the conference room with his three sons and Naya. When he heard footsteps coming from behind him, he didn't need to turn and look to know who was there.

At least her bodyguard, Grigori, was with her. "Mother."

"Boris, let's not waste time with you blustering about the bunker. The threat looks like it has been neutralized. Fill me in on what you know."

"How is Marrick?" Naya asked.

"Sabrina's running a bunch of tests right now. It will be a while until we know anything," Irina said. "What do you think happened?"

"I'm not sure," Naya said. "The portal seems to have jammed. Energy flows from earth to the realm, and when the portal opens, you ride the energy from one reality to another. But something stopped it and shoved Marrick back through and out again when the connection was blocked."

"What could cause that?" Boris asked.

"I don't know," Naya said.

"Do you think we're under attack?" Aleksei asked.

"Possibly, but if that's the case, then why didn't any realm demons come through the portal?"

"Maybe they can't," Irina said.

"What are you thinking, Babushka?" Aleksei asked.

"We thought the opposition was over, but maybe we were too optimistic. What if they found a way to block the portal?"

"Is that possible?" Boris asked Naya.

"Anything is possible. We won't know unless we try to open a portal again."

Aleksei frowned. "I don't think it's a good idea."

"I wouldn't enter it, but I could try to activate it," Naya reassured Aleksei. "There's an initial pulse before the portal opens, and I'll shut it down at that point."

"Let's do it," Boris said. "Grigori."

Grigori nodded and escorted Irina out of the room. And for once Irina didn't argue with him. If they weren't in the middle of a crisis and he had time to think, her acquiescence would make him nervous.

Naya concentrated for several minutes. The longer she tried, the further Boris's stomach dropped.

Naya shook her head. "I can't open the portal. I'll try to reach the realm guards telepathically and find out what's going on, but it might take some time."

Aleksei cursed. "We're supposed to be bringing the next group to earth in two weeks."

Boris rested his hand on Aleksei's shoulder. "We'll figure it out. In the meantime, I'm going to keep the extra guards in place around the compound. Misha, did you contact the BSR team?"

"Yes, they're on the way here."

"Okay, let's keep the clan in the bunker for a little longer until we talk through next steps. And let's move this to the hospital conference room so we can find out how Marrick is doing. Maybe he has a sense of what happened."

They headed into the hallway. While his family went to the hospital, Boris stayed behind and spoke to two guards, who stationed themselves in the room in case a portal appeared. He also spoke to the head guard and quickly discussed increasing security.

He finally made his way down the hall of the hospital and entered the conference room, where his family waited for him around a large table. A whiteboard was on one wall, and a screen where Misha could display his computer or tablet screen to the group was on the other end of the room.

Aleksei was talking on his phone while pacing back and forth at the front of the room, and from what Boris could hear, he was talking to Doyle, who worked for Aleksei on the migration team.

Sergei came into the room. "I told one of the nurses they can find us in here whenever they have news or questions about Marrick."

Boris nodded.

The door opened and Kyle burst into the room in her usual style, followed by the rest of the BSR team. Vampires and mates Jean-Luc and Talia strolled in, followed by human-shifter Jason, and Kyle's mate, who Kyle called by his last name, Dalton, but everyone else called Joe.

"How's Marrick?" Kyle asked.

"We don't know much yet. Hopefully Sabrina will be here soon," Misha said as he held out his hands for the backpack Jean Luc brought for him. Misha unzipped it and pulled out a laptop and a tablet.

Aleksei ended his call. "I just talked to Doyle. He's going to talk to some of his contacts on the street to see if they've heard anything."

Talia spoke up. "We also called Sylvia while we were on the way here. She's going to talk to some of the realm demons living in her building to see if they've heard about any issues."

Sylvia was a human woman who helped realm demons acclimate to earth. Many months ago she had helped the BSR team understand about the demons being forced into indentured servitude in exchange for their passage to earth, telling them it was time to come up with a legitimate way to bring demons to earth, and the realm migration was born.

Boris passed the head of the table and sat down on the right side. Aleksei looked at him and Boris nodded slightly.

Aleksei sat there instead. He brought the BSR team up to speed, and they were just starting to talk about options when Sabrina joined them.

Naya stood up from her seat to Aleksei's left. "How is he?"

"For now Marrick is stable. He has a sprained arm that should only need a couple of days to mend, and luckily his head wound is superficial. He's going to be really sore from slamming into the wall as hard as he did, but he has no neck or back injuries."

"What do you mean, 'for now'?" Naya asked. Aleksei went over and put his arm around her.

Sabrina frowned, which was never a good sign. "He's still unconscious, and his energy pattern is unlike anything I've ever felt before. I don't know what's going on with it, and it's not something I can test for." She turned to Sergei. "It would help if Lela could examine him. She has a way of looking inside people to read their energy. Maybe she can help."

"I was going to have the compound reduce the alarm to a level two. Let everyone out of the bunkers but have them stay in their homes for at least tonight," Boris said. "Sergei, why don't you go get Lela? Misha, I know you want to take Callie and the boys home."

Misha and Sergei both stood.

"I'll be back as soon as I can," Misha said. "Callie and the boys will be more than happy to watch Kara for a while, yes?"

Naya seemed to relax. "Thanks, that would be very helpful. Sabrina, when can I see Marrick?"

"I'll let you see him in a few minutes, okay?"

Naya nodded, and Aleksei kissed her temple before they took their seats again.

Boris looked around the table at his family and friends. It was time to figure out what had happened and put a stop to it, both for his clan, and for all the realm demons who wanted to come to earth.

Chapter 7

Sam checked the monitors and made a note on Marrick's chart. His skin color was a little darker, but not purple enough that she felt better about it. She'd been relieved when the scans all came back negative on his neck, back, and head.

But she didn't understand why he was still unconscious and neither did Sabrina.

Sam might think of the doctor as Sabrina, but in the hospital setting she would be calling her Dr. Miller. It was hard-coded into her, and she wouldn't change anytime soon. But from what she had seen so far, Sabrina was top-notch, and someone she was proud to work for.

She rested her hand on Marrick's arm and leaned close to his ear. "You're safe here. You're in the hospital and we're taking care of you."

"Any change?" Sabrina asked as she joined Sam.

"His pressure seems to be stabilizing a little more, but everything else is the same."

"Lela should be here soon."

"Is she a healer?"

Sabrina nodded. "In a matter of speaking. Lela is a Kelmar, one of the most powerful demon clans in the realm. She has the ability to sense energy blockages in people and help determine what's wrong with them."

"Wow."

"Are you ready to be relieved? You weren't exactly scheduled to work today."

Sam shook her head. "I'm fine. I'd like to be here when Lela checks him, if it's okay."

Sabrina nodded while reviewing his chart and called for another bag of saline to keep him hydrated. By the time Sam had it hooked to his IV, Lela was standing in the doorway.

"Thanks for coming," Sabrina said, backing away from Marrick, so Sam did the same.

Lela studied Marrick, letting her gaze move slowly from the top of his head down to his toes and then back up his body again.

Once they confirmed he didn't have a back or neck injury, they had removed his armor-plated uniform. But it didn't make him look smaller. The orderlies had to hunt before they found a big enough hospital gown and helped put it on him.

Sam took a shallow breath after she realized she had been holding it while Lela stood there saying nothing. Finally Lela blinked and focused on Sabrina.

"What do you think?" Sabrina asked.

"His energy is depleted. It's not flowing the way it should."

"Where?" Sabrina asked.

Lela frowned. "That's the thing. It's everywhere. I think it's down to the cellular level."

That couldn't be good.

"Can you explain to me what you see?" Sabrina said.

"His cells are all out of sync. Like he's partly here and partly elsewhere, if that makes sense. Like they're struggling to exist in the same space."

"Like the bends," Sam said.

"Exactly," Sabrina responded.

Lela looked from one to the other of them in confusion.

Sam explained. "People who dive deep in the ocean have to come up slowly or the nitrogen in their body flows into their bloodstream and causes problems. If that happens, you have to put them in a chamber that mimics the pressure in the ocean and then slowly decrease the pressure to release the nitrogen from the bloodstream."

"Correct," Sabrina said. "We don't know exactly what going through the portal does to you at a molecular level. And Marrick was partially through the process and then thrown back out of the portal before it finished."

"So we should send him back through the portal," Sam said.

Lela shook her head. "We can't."

"Why not?" Sabrina asked.

"Sergei told me Naya already tried to open the portal again and it didn't work. Right now there's no way to get to the realm."

Sam's stomach twisted. What could they do for him?

Sabrina took a step closer to Marrick and watched the monitor above his bed for a moment before speaking. "Until we can get him through the portal, we need to do something to stabilize him. Lela, do you think you can push some of your energy into him and see if you can adjust his cells a bit?"

"I can try."

Lela placed one hand on his forehead and the other on his chest and closed her eyes for several minutes. Sam didn't dare say a word, so she just stood there waiting.

Finally Lela opened her eyes. "I think I helped a little, but I can't heal him, Sabrina. The damage is pretty severe."

Sabrina nodded. "As long as it buys us some time until we get the portal open again."

After a couple minutes, Sabrina walked Lela out to talk to Boris, Aleksei, and the others.

Sam took a damp cloth and wiped it over Marrick's forehead. When she removed it, she was surprised to see his yellow eyes looking up at her.

"Welcome back," she said.

He blinked and attempted to look around.

"You're okay. You're still on earth, in the compound hospital. There was an accident with the portal, and you were hurt."

"Others okay?" he asked in a rusty voice.

"Everyone else is fine. Don't try to talk too much yet."

He looked down at his wrapped arm.

"The wrapping is for your sprained arm, and you probably have a headache from the bump on your head. Are you in pain anywhere else?"

"No."

Sabrina came back through the door and beamed when she saw Marrick was awake. "Look who decided to join us. How are you feeling?"

"Okay."

Sabrina rested her hand on his arm. "Do you feel dizzy?"

He frowned up at her.

"Is the room spinning, or does your head hurt?" she clarified.

"No."

"I told him about his arm and head injury," Sam said. "Can I give him a sip of water?"

"Yes. I'll be right back," Sabrina said on her way out of the room.

Sam got a cup of water and a straw and held it down so Marrick could take a sip.

"Easy. Not too much."

He rested his head back against the pillow. "Thanks."

Sabrina walked back in with Naya, who gave Marrick's hand a reassuring squeeze. "About time you woke up."

Marrick gripped her hand. "Is Kara okay?"

Naya's eyes softened on him. "Yes. She's being spoiled right now by Callie and the twins while we try to figure out what happened. Can you tell me what you remember?"

"Everything was fine at first. I stepped into the portal, and got to the point where you feel like you can't take your next breath."

That was what it felt like to go through the portal?

Naya nodded as if what he said made perfect sense.

"But then I couldn't move forward. I was stuck, and the pressure pushed down on me. Just when I thought my chest would explode, I was jerked through the air...and I don't remember much after that."

He looked up at Sam, and she realized she'd been resting her hand on his shoulder while he was talking.

Sabrina and Naya exchanged a look.

"What aren't you telling me?" Marrick said.

"Since you were in the middle of transporting to the realm and then thrown back to earth, the energy and cells in your body are now out of sync...like they need to finish the transition."

"So I'll just go through the portal," Marrick said.

"I think it would help, yes," Sabrina replied.

"Except right now we can't get the portal to open. It stopped working when the accident occurred," Naya said.

Marrick closed his eyes for a moment, and Sam, Naya, and Sabrina exchanged looks.

Marrick opened his eyes again. "Maybe I'm the one who needs to activate it. If my jump didn't finish, maybe I locked it down somehow."

"That could be possible," Naya said.

"So let's try," he said, and moved as if to sit up.

Sam put both hands on his chest. "Whoa. Not so fast."

"Sam's right," Sabrina said. "You need to take it easy for a bit."

"We can't wait. If I can fix the portal, we need to do it as soon as possible."

Naya squeezed his hand. "Agreed. But I need to discuss this with Aleksei and Boris, and find out where they want us to try this. We need a safe place. Give me a few minutes."

Marrick nodded and relaxed against the pillow, and Sam could tell just that little bit of movement had tired him.

Sabrina watched the monitors for a few moments. "Are you tired, Marrick?"

"Yes."

"It might help if you take your human form. On earth it takes more energy to hold your demon form in place."

He closed his eyes and his body changed before Sam's eyes. Tan skin and black hair appeared. He opened his eyes, and their blue—almost violet—gaze punched Sam in the gut. She'd admired them before, but being so close packed an extra wallop.

He sighed.

"Did that help?" Sabrina asked.

"A little, yes."

"Sam and I are going to leave the room for a couple of minutes. I want you to close your eyes and rest while we wait for Naya to get back."

They left the room, and Sam glanced back to make sure he was resting before closing the door.

"You're a good nurse," Sabrina said. "Actually, I take it back. You're a great nurse."

Heat rushed up Sam's neck into her face.

"Thanks." She cleared her throat. "I'm worried about him."

Sabrina's smile faded. "Me too. But we don't know what this means yet. We'll take it one step at a time while we work on opening the portal to send him through."

"And if he can't?"

"Maybe the longer he stays on earth, the more his cells will adjust to this side of the portal."

Sam nodded, although she wasn't convinced. She didn't understand why all her alarm bells were ringing, but they were. She always trusted her gut, and her gut was telling her this was the beginning of something very, very bad.

Normally when she got this feeling, it was time to make a run for it. But for once she was hesitating. Why, she didn't know, since she'd only been in Cleveland for a few days. Certainly not enough time to form attachments.

But something was telling her, loud and clear, that she shouldn't run.

At least not yet.

CHAPTER 8

Marrick half closed his eyes and watched Sam and Sabrina leave. He also saw Sam turn around and look at him before shutting the door.

Sam confused him. She had the heart of a healer, and he'd felt her compassion and concern, but there was still an underlying hint of fear. But now he'd transitioned into his human form? The fear had almost disappeared.

She was scared of his demon form. But why?

He wanted to figure it out, especially after she'd laid her hand on his shoulder and then on his chest. The heat of her hands had calmed him. But before he could explore that, he needed to fix the portal. He didn't need his empathic senses to tell him everyone was worried. If the portal was broken, they had no way to bring the realm demons to earth. That was the priority, even if going through the portal didn't fix whatever was wrong with him.

And based on Sabrina's explanation and the collective worry he sensed from Naya and Sam—for some reason he couldn't read Sabrina—he knew he was in trouble.

But he'd been raised a warrior. And warriors knew sacrifice might be necessary in order to protect others.

He opened his eyes, sat up, and swung his legs over the side of the bed. The room spun for a moment, and he took a deep breath. Where were his clothes?

"What do you think you're doing, buster?"

He turned toward the voice and found Sam standing in the door with fire in her eyes.

"My name is Marrick, not Buster."

Sam rolled her eyes at him. "I know your name is Marrick. Buster is just a saying."

He couldn't stifle his grin.

Her eyes narrowed on him before a smirk tilted her lips. "You already know what it means."

"I do." For some reason he couldn't resist teasing her.

"Don't try to distract me. Why are you trying to get up?"

"I need to change my clothes." He looked down at the blue cloth he had on. "This is not going to work when I go through the portal."

"I need to take your IV out first. Hold on a second."

She must be talking about the tube sticking out of his arm. That was what Sabrina had called it last time, when Naya was sick and he brought her to the hospital.

Sam reached for some of the clear coverings for her hands and slipped them on, then leaned over and pulled the sticky white strips off his arm and gently removed the thin metal, then pressed down on the spot with a white square.

"There. Let me put some tape over this gauze." She patted his arm when she was done. "I'll go get your clothes and one of the orderlies who can help you get dressed."

He couldn't keep the frown off his face. "I can dress myself."

Her mouth quirked up on the right side. "Either the orderly helps you, or you can walk around in the hospital gown. Which can get quite chilly, just so you know."

"Fine."

Her grin spread before she stepped out of the room and closed the door. A few minutes later a male by the name of Jim helped him steady himself and pull on his clothes. It was hard to maneuver around the wrapped arm. And when

Marrick realized the back of the gown was open except for a few ties, he laughed.

So Sam was going to let him walk around in this? She was a feisty one. He liked it when she wasn't scared of him.

He put on his armor and took a deep breath to calm his heart. He hoped he could open the portal and put everything right again.

Jim opened the door for him, and Marrick walked out into the hall and headed toward some familiar voices.

Pausing in the doorway, he saw a room with a large table and several people sitting or standing around it. Earth had a lot of these kinds of rooms, although he wasn't exactly sure why they needed to conference so much.

Boris, Aleksei, Naya, Sergei, Misha, and the BSR team were sitting around the table as Sabrina and Sam stood at the head of the table.

"Look who's up," someone said cheerfully, and he looked toward the voice to see Irina was here as well.

Aleksei stood up. "Good to see you, my friend."

"And you. Has Naya told you of my plan?"

Boris nodded. "Yes. After the last time, we were just talking about a safe place to try opening the portal again. I think we should do it in the backup bunker."

"We have a backup bunker?" Misha asked.

Boris smiled. "I'm all about contingencies. We have six active bunkers, plus a seventh one if needed. Let's try it there. The walls are two feet thick."

Everyone stood up at once.

Boris held up his hands. "Oh, no, you are not all coming to the bunker. Besides Marrick, who needs to be there?" He looked around the room.

Naya spoke up. "I'm going. I can help contain things if there are any more surprises."

"Agreed," Boris said, "which means Aleksei is coming with us, since I don't have time to fight him on this."

"Very true," Aleksei said.

"Misha, you and the team will be on standby in case we need to move the clan back to the bunkers."

"I'm going too," Sabrina said.

"Me too," Sam chimed in.

"It might not be safe," Marrick said.

Boris narrowed his eyes at Sam and Sabrina. "You both can wait outside the bunker with me until Aleksei and Naya give us the all clear."

Before either female could respond, Boris clapped his hands together. "Okay, that's settled. Let's make this happen."

"Let's make this happen?" Kyle echoed.

Boris gave her a crooked smile. "Sorry, I've always wanted to say that."

Marrick followed Boris, Aleksei, Naya, Sabrina, and Sam outside to a white box with wheels and a red cross on the side.

Sabrina opened the side like a door to a house. "This is an ambulance. It lets us transport people who need urgent medical care."

He nodded and got in, even though he didn't know exactly what to make of it.

"Trust me, I know what you're thinking. It's okay." Naya said before climbing in along with Aleksei and Sam. Sabrina opened another door and climbed into a chair, while Boris climbed into the other side. Was he going to operate this thing?

Marrick blew out a breath as the box started to rattle and they moved forward! He glanced at Naya and Aleksei, who were relaxing on seats to the side. He and Sam were sitting on a bed. Why was there a bed in the back?

In a matter of minutes, they stopped, and everyone climbed out and gathered next to a large door in the ground leading down into the earth.

"Good luck," Sam said as Aleksei, Naya, and Marrick headed down the stairs.

Why was he nervous? He opened the portal all the time. He could do it now. Although he wasn't sure what would happen if he entered it again. The last time had been far from pleasant.

He stood in the middle of the space and concentrated. And concentrated some more.

Nothing. After several long, drawn-out minutes, still nothing. He shook his head.

Aleksei ran up the stairs and opened the door. Moments later Boris, Sabrina, and Sam joined them.

"It didn't work," he said, and began to sway.

Naya grabbed his good arm.

"Whoa. Why don't you sit down for a moment?" Sam encouraged him.

He frowned. "I don't know why I'm dilly."

"It's 'dizzy,' and you just expended quite a bit of energy trying to open the portal," Sabrina said as she squatted down in front of him, closed her eyes, and held her hands above his head.

After a few moments she opened them again. "I still sense the same disjointed energy. I think you need to come back to the hospital."

"And do what?" Marrick said.

"We'll run some more tests and see if we can do something to help you."

His gut told him there was nothing she could do. "We need to figure out who's blocking the portal."

Boris held up his hands in front of him. "I'll make a deal with you. You go to the hospital tonight and let Sabrina run some tests. Tomorrow you can be a part of the team figuring out what's going on, and you can stay at my house until we resolve this. I practically live across the street from the hospital." He looked at Sabrina. "Which means you can come and check on him if needed. We are agreed, yes?"

Marrick blinked. "Now I know where Aleksei gets his negotiating skills."

"I'm not sure that was a compliment," Aleksei said.

"Of course it was a compliment, Son," Boris said.

Marrick glanced over at Sam, who looked like she was trying not to laugh, and then he couldn't stifle his own grin. It was good to smile in the face of whatever was coming—and something was coming—so if he found lightness in the eyes of a caring female, he would welcome it.

CHAPTER 9

Sam changed into her pajamas and climbed into one of the twin beds. She took a couple of deep breaths and tried to relax, but adrenaline was still pulsing through her from earlier.

Throwing back the covers, she reached for her duffel and dug to the bottom to pull out her doll. Yes, she knew it was ridiculous for a one-hundred-and-fifty-seven-year-old to still have a doll, but it was the only thing she had left from her past. The past before their lives changed irrevocably.

There was something about this ratty doll that gave her peace. Fates love her mother, she had never raised an eye about Sam's need to keep this doll. Never once asked her when she was going to throw it away.

And now she was missing her mother. She picked up the burner phone and sent a simple one-word text. Her phone rang seconds later. She should have known her mother would call her.

"Hello. Didn't know if you were awake or not."

"I'm always available to talk, any time you want. Did you get the job?"

"Yes."

"That's great! Why don't you sound more excited? Is something wrong?" her mom asked.

"Yes...no. I'm fine."

"Further explanation is needed."

Sam could just see her mother's serious expression.

"I'm fine. But something happened to Marrick."

"The portal guard you talked about before?"

"Yes." Sam told her what happened. To her mother's credit, she didn't waste time on disbelief. Instead she jumped right in, asking questions so she could better understand the situation.

"So how's Marrick now?"

"Still the same. Sabrina ran some more tests, and then he finally fell asleep."

"Did the tests help you figure out how to help him?"

"Not yet."

"You'll figure it out. And it sounds like this clan will figure out how to open the portal again."

"You sound pretty optimistic when you haven't met any of them."

"True, but based on what you've told me, this clan loves each other. Not something we've seen much of in our lives, Sam, but I think they'll figure this out."

"For Marrick's sake, I hope you're right."

"It sounds like you took charge earlier tonight when he was hurt."

Sam shrugged, and then reminded herself her mother couldn't see her. "My training kicked in."

"Don't downplay your talent, Sam. I'm proud of you."

Heat rushed up Sam's neck into her face. "Thanks." Sam blinked up at the ceiling. "I thought this conversation was going to go differently."

"What do you mean?"

"I thought you would tell me to leave." They had been on the run, avoiding...things...for so long. And now Sam had been thrown into the middle of something unknown.

"What do you want to do?" her mom asked.

"I want to stick it out for now."

"Agreed. But you'll be ready to leave if you have to, right?"

"Yes. I'm going to try and get some sleep. I want to be back at the hospital early."

"I wouldn't think Sabrina would make you work tomorrow."

"I'm not on the schedule," Sam said as she pulled the covers up over her.

Silence.

"Are you still there, Mom?" Sam asked.

"It's good of you to want to check on Marrick. He sounds like a good male."

Sam's heartbeat sped up. "I was the one on the scene when he was hurt. I want to help if I can."

"Of course. Get some sleep, sweetheart."

Sam didn't like how quickly her mother agreed with her. Normally her mother challenged her on a daily basis, and often more than once a day.

But Sam didn't have enough energy to think about it. There'd been enough emotional upheaval today. Tomorrow was a new day. She settled down in the bed and closed her eyes. She would stick around for now. After all, she was an expert at dropping everything and leaving.

But for some reason, even though she'd only been there for a couple days, the idea of leaving didn't appeal to her. She wanted to help. Wanted to feel a part of something. Wanted to make a difference somehow, and in some way.

———◆○◆———

It felt like Sam had just closed her eyes when the morning light beamed through the windows and woke her up. She wanted to pull the covers over her head, but she got up instead and walked with Irina to the community center.

Apparently Irina often made breakfast for the night-shift guards, and since there had been more guards than usual on duty last night, Irina was on a mission.

Today's mission involved breakfast sandwiches.

She helped Irina for a little bit, but Irina obviously was used to doing this on her own. The female could easily feed an army if she put her mind to it.

"Good morning," Boris said as he joined them in the kitchen.

Several of the guards stood straighter when he entered the room.

Boris gestured for them to go back to their meals. "Relax and enjoy your breakfast. I just came to thank you all for being on call last night and stepping up to guard the compound. I think it calls for two sandwiches each."

The guards chuckled, and Irina put her hands on her hips with a twinkle in her eye. "Are you going to roll up your sleeves and help? I'm going to need someone to make more biscuits."

"Why of course, Mother. Tell me what needs to be done."

Irina huffed at him playfully. "I think I have it under control."

"I'm sure you do." He looked at Sam. "I'm surprised you're up after your late night."

"I'm heading to the hospital next to check on Marrick."

"I'm heading to the hospital myself. I told Marrick he can stay with me until we figure things out."

"Hold up, Son," Irina said. "I'm wrapping up some sandwiches for the hospital staff. Sam can walk over with you and hand out the sandwiches while I finish up here."

After a couple of minutes, they went out the side door of the community center toward the hospital. Boris reached for Sam's basket of sandwiches.

"Let me."

Sam cleared her throat. "Your clan is very lucky to live here."

"Thank you. We've worked hard to make sure the clan is taken care of, whether they live in the compound or not."

She looked over at him. "You allow clan members to live outside the compound?"

"Yes. Until recently, Aleksei was my only son who lived in the compound. Misha had an apartment in Cleveland, and Sergei traveled all over the world taking pictures."

The front door of the hospital slid open, and they walked up to the front desk.

"Hello, Corinne," Boris said. "I hear you have a new addition to your family."

Corinne beamed. "Grandbaby number three. She's gorgeous."

"Congratulations. Make sure to e-mail a picture to Irina or I'll never hear the end of it. Have you met Sam yet?"

"No. I wasn't on duty last night, but I've heard good things about you. Welcome, Sam."

Sam's face heated. "Nice to meet you. Irina sent over some breakfast sandwiches for the team."

Corinne's eyes lit up. "I knew I smelled something yummy. Let me show you where the staff lounge is, and I'll let everyone know they're here."

Sam turned to Boris, and he handed her the basket.

"Thank you."

He nodded. "I'm going to check on Marrick."

"Marrick is in room twelve," Corinne said.

"Thanks." He looked at Sam. "I'll see you later, yes?"

She smiled at him before she followed Corinne to the staff lounge.

———————◆◇◆———————

Marrick sat on the bed as he awkwardly fastened the last tie on his uniform. Having his arm wrapped slowed him down, but Sabrina told him his arm should be healed shortly.

Unlike the rest of him. Sabrina hadn't said that, but he knew it to be the case. He didn't feel right, and was unsteady at times, as if his skin didn't fit his body anymore.

A sound had him turning. Boris stood in the doorway.

"Good to see you up. How are you feeling?"

"Better."

"I figured you'd be ready to break out of here as soon as possible, so I got here early."

Marrick tilted his head at Boris's comment. "Have I been under arrest?"

Boris chuckled. "No. That's just an expression. It means you really want to leave."

"Ahh. Yes, I want to break out of here. Have we found out anything about the portal?"

"Not yet," Boris said, shaking his head. "We're going to talk to the team later this morning. They're trying to find out if their contacts know anything about who, or what, could be blocking the portal."

"Has Naya talked to any of the guards?"

"She was having difficulty reaching anyone last night. I'm going to call her in a few minutes and see if she's had any luck. Are you ready to leave?"

"Yes," Marrick said.

"No," a voice said from behind Boris.

Sam stalked into the room, frowning. "Has Sabrina agreed to discharge you?"

Marrick shrugged. "I don't know what discharge even means."

"It means she said it's okay for you to leave the hospital."

Marrick stood. "Boris is breaking me out of here."

The frown that had been directed at him was now directed at Boris. "Really?"

Boris smiled, and her eyes narrowed on him further.

"Of course we will confirm with Sabrina before leaving. I assumed, since he is dressed, that he was given the green light."

Marrick headed toward the door. "Why would Sabrina give me a light that is green? You all speak in riddles. Are you ready to go, Boris?"

Luckily Sabrina was heading toward them in the hall. Otherwise he was afraid Sam would have blocked the doorway to stop him from leaving.

"Dr. Miller. Are you okay with Marrick leaving?" Sam asked.

Sabrina stopped in front of them. "I think it's okay for him to stay with Boris for now." She pierced Marrick with a look. "But you need to take it easy. Can you do that?"

"Yes," Marrick said at the same time Sam let out a huff.

"I'll take care of him, Sabrina," Boris volunteered.

"I'll hold you to that," Sabrina said. "We'll want to check on you periodically, Marrick."

"Thank you for your help." Then he looked at Sam. "My thanks to both of you for taking care of me."

Sam's eyes widened. "You're welcome."

Marrick gave her a quick nod before he and Boris headed out of the hospital and down the street. There was something so compelling and yet confusing about Sam. But now was not the time to think about it. Not when he didn't know what his future held. Or if he had a future at all.

"We're going to my house first. You'll stay with me until we can open the portal again."

Marrick looked around as they walked.

"It's a lot to take in, yes?"

"It's so different from the in-between and the realm."

"Yes. Feel free to ask me questions about anything."

"I have so many questions, I don't know where to begin."

Boris clamped his hand on his shoulder for a moment. "Then it's a good thing I love to talk."

Marrick smiled at him.

Boris pointed. "This is my home here."

When they walked in, Marrick paused at the door. "You have all of this, and you live here by yourself?"

"Yes. My sons have been grown for a while now. It's just me." Boris took him through the house and answered all his questions.

When they walked through the space Boris called a living room into another room, Marrick stopped.

"You have a room just for your table?"

"It seems silly when you put it that way. But yes. When I have the family come together for meals, we use this room—the dining room. Now all three of my sons are mated, dinners are quite entertaining."

"It's good to have family."

Boris nodded. "Yes. What about you, Marrick? Where's your family?"

"My parents are both gone now. I was born in the in-between and followed their path by becoming a portal guard."

Boris paused. "Have you thought about what you'll do once the migration is complete?"

Marrick shrugged. "I haven't made plans yet. I want to ensure those who wish to come to earth are able to do so. That's my priority right now."

Marrick looked up at the painting hanging above the fireplace. It was a painting of Boris, Misha as a young man, two younger boys—one with dark hair who must be Aleksei, one with blond hair, Sergei—and a female. Naya had told him Boris's mate passed on years ago.

"Sergei looks like your mate."

"He does, especially through the eyes. Anna loved the boys very much. She said they were our greatest accomplishment."

"Your sons are good males. Even Aleksei, who I was concerned about at first."

Boris turned away from the painting. "Aleksei needed someone to balance him, and Naya is his perfect mate."

"She is. I told her more than once that they belonged together, but she needed to figure it out on her own. Stubborn."

Boris chuckled as they entered yet another room. "This is the kitchen, and it's probably the scariest room in the house." Boris showed Marrick the pantry and a large box he called a refrigerator.

"Amazing."

"Yes. And you don't have to light a fire to cook." He turned the burner on the stove and Marrick gaped at it. "Okay, that's enough for now. I don't want to overwhelm you right out of the hospital. I'd never hear the end of it from Sabrina and Sam."

Marrick shook his head. "I thought Naya was strong-willed."

Boris led him down the hall to a bedroom. "You'll stay here."

"Knock knock," a voice called out.

"Come in, Misha. We're in the guest room."

Misha entered the room carrying a duffel. "How are you feeling, Marrick?"

"Better."

Misha held up the bag. "I brought you some clothes to wear while you're here."

Marrick frowned, and Boris spoke up. "You and Misha are about the same size, and there's no reason for you to wear the uniform while you're here."

Marrick decided not to fight them on this, since they were *all* stubborn. "Thank you."

"Do you need Misha or me to explain any of the clothes fasteners to you?"

Marrick shook his head. "No. I've seen the clothes you have been sending to the realm in the supplies. I understand how the zippers and buttons work."

"Have you not taken any for yourself?" Boris asked.

"Others need the clothes more. I have my uniform."

Boris gazed at him for a drawn-out moment before turning to Misha. "Have we heard anything yet?" Boris asked.

"Kyle and Jason are with Sylvia right now to find out what intel she's been able to gather from the realm demon connections she has on earth," Misha said. "Callie will be here shortly, right after she drops Matty and Luke at school."

"Okay. Aleksei and Naya should be here shortly as well. Hopefully Naya was able to communicate with someone in the realm to find out what's going on there."

"We need to figure this out, and fast," Misha said.

"We will, Son. We stopped the naysayers on earth and the realm in the past and we'll do it again."

At a knock at the front door, Misha and Boris left Marrick alone to change clothes. He fumbled with them for a couple of minutes and pulled on a pair of blue pants made out of a heavy material and a soft shirt with three buttons at the neck. Luckily there was enough give in the material to fit over his arm.

He left the bedroom and followed the voices until he saw that Aleksei, Naya, and Callie had also arrived.

Naya checked him from head to toe and then smiled at him. "Well don't you look like an earther," she said.

Marrick looked down at himself. "Is that a good thing?"

Boris chuckled. "Why don't we move to the dining room to talk through what we've found out so far."

Marrick nodded, forcing back a huff of impatience. He was a male of action. All this talking was not solving their problem. And they needed to get the portal back up and running again for everyone's sake.

CHAPTER 10

Marrick looked around the table at this proud family working so hard to fix things. He cleared his throat. "Naya, were you able to contact the guards?"

"Yes. The realm is okay. Nothing has happened, and they aren't under attack."

"But?" Marrick said.

"But after I spoke with Krell, he tried to open the portal on his side, and nothing happened."

Misha frowned. "I had hoped if someone was able to open it in the realm, it might fix the issue."

Boris sighed. "So did I."

"Have you ever heard of this happening before, Father?" Aleksei asked.

"No. And the portal has been functioning since before the clans were sent to the realm more than a millennium ago."

"Could this be a malfunction of some sort?" Callie asked.

"Possibly. But my gut tells me someone has blocked it. We still have dissenters." Boris turned to Marrick. "Are there demons in the realm still opposed to immigration?"

"There might be. But since Aleksei came to the realm and we now have supplies coming from earth, the healing centers, and the mentors teaching the realm about earth, we haven't heard much grumbling."

"I wish the same could be said about earth," Boris said. "Has Doyle heard anything?"

"Nothing beyond the normal protestors," Aleksei said.

"Hopefully Sylvia's heard something. Can you call Kyle and see if they have anything to add?"

Misha pulled something out of his pocket and pushed his finger on the shiny surface.

Marrick frowned at the ringing noise coming from the flat box.

Naya leaned over and whispered in his ear. "That's a phone. It's a communication device."

"Hey, Mish."

Marrick jumped at the sound of Kyle's voice coming from the device.

"Kyle, I have you on speaker, and everyone is here. Have you guys hooked up with Sylvia yet?"

"They sure have, big boy." Another voice came out of the flat rectangle. How did they do this? "How's married life treating you?"

Misha beamed. "Married life is great. It's good to hear your voice, Sylvia. Sorry it's under these circumstances."

"It's never dull, that's for sure. I've put some feelers out to see if there's been any chatter."

Feelers? Chatter? What language was this female speaking?

"Heard anything back yet?" Misha asked.

"No. But it's still early. The team and I are going to go talk to a couple of demons."

"Are you aware of any Abstatholm on earth who we could talk to?" Aleksei asked.

Marrick agreed with Aleksei's question since Abstatholm were high-level Kelmar who had the ability to travel through space and could open the portal on their own, without the help of the portal devices. Maybe they knew what had happened to the portal.

"We don't have that many Kelmar who were brought here illegally," Sylvia said.

"Makes sense. The ones forcing the demons into indentured service wouldn't have wanted other powerful demons coming to earth and possibly overthrowing them," Kyle said.

Kyle and Sylvia said goodbye, and Misha put the flat box into his pocket again.

"We should ask Lela to see if she can talk to the Kelmar who've come here as part of the migration. Maybe they can help with this. Where are Sergei and Lela this morning?" Boris asked.

"They're scheduled to move out of their apartment today into their new house," Callie said.

"That's right." Boris smiled.

Misha chuckled. "Get that smug smile off your face."

Boris's smile expanded into a grin. "I'm allowed to be happy because my sons are close by."

Callie elbowed Misha. "Yes, you are."

"In the meantime, what else should we be doing?" Boris asked.

Naya spoke up. "Krell is reaching out to the realm clan leaders to tell them what's happened."

"Is that wise?" Boris asked.

"We don't want to keep anything from them. If we did, we'd destroy the trust we've built with the clans," Aleksei said.

"Plus, the guards are going to start investigating as well. We don't know who did this. Is it someone in the realm or on earth?" Naya asked.

"Or both?" Marrick added.

Boris frowned. "Speaking of telling the truth, I'm going to have to tell the Demon Council what happened."

Aleksei cursed.

"My feelings exactly, Son. But we can't keep it from them. I'm going to schedule a call with them tonight. If I wait any longer, they'll think we're trying to hide something."

Aleksei sighed. "We're going to keep moving forward with the migration. I don't want us to stop the momentum. When we get this figured out, I want to be able to still bring the demons to earth."

"Agreed," Boris said. "Callie, if you need extra hands, let us know, okay?"

Callie stood up. "Thanks. I'll let you know. I'm heading to the office now."

Misha stood up. "I'll head out with you. I'm going to dig into some of the demon sites online to see if I can find anything about someone blocking the portal."

"I should be getting back to the office with Callie," Aleksei said.

Boris nodded. "I'm going to step across the hall into my office, Marrick, and schedule the call for tonight. You'll be okay for a bit?"

"I'll stay here for a while," Naya said.

After everyone said their goodbyes, Marrick turned to his friend. "You don't have to watch over me like I'm a babe. I'm fine."

Naya patted his shoulder. "I know. But I also remember how overwhelming it was when I first came to earth. So you need to take it slow for a bit."

"We can't afford to take it slow."

"You're frustrated."

He looked at her but didn't answer.

"It's okay. In the realm we use action more than words. Here on earth, it's much more complicated. We can't just swoop in and fix things. We have to figure out who's behind this and stop them."

Marrick sighed. "I don't like not being in control."

"I get it. But until we know more, there isn't much swooping to be done."

"Who are you, and what have you done with Naya?"

She laughed. "I was the hothead of the two of us, wasn't I?"

"Yes."

"I had to learn to take it one step at a time, or frustration was my constant companion. Plus, I have a baby. If that doesn't teach you patience, nothing will."

Marrick swallowed. "I'm so happy for you, Naya."

She grabbed his hand and squeezed it. "Thank you. I'm one lucky female to have Kara and a mate like Aleksei."

Marrick chuckled. "Which is pretty funny, considering you couldn't tolerate him at first."

"True. But he showed me what a wonderful mate he is. I hope someday you find someone special."

"I've never dared hope for a mate."

"None of us did, but once the realm migration finishes, the portal guards can come to earth as well. Have you thought about what you want to do?"

He shook his head. "I haven't given it much thought."

"Well, you could settle here. You would be welcomed by the clan." She gave him a nudge with her elbow. "And I've seen the way you look at Sam."

"She doesn't like me."

"Really? Well, she doesn't act like someone who hates you."

"What do you mean?"

"When the portal malfunctioned, Aleksei ordered everyone out of the conference room and set the emergency protocol to lock down the room. When you flew out of the portal and slammed into the wall, Sam ran back into the room to help you."

"What?"

"She worked on you while we stood guard at the portal. At one point the portal made a horrific noise, and Sam threw herself over you to protect you."

Marrick's stomach dropped. "She could have been hurt!"

"She was doing her job."

"She's a caretaker, not a soldier."

"You know healers often have to work in the thick of battle. They're as heroic as the soldiers battling around them." She looked at him for a moment. "I didn't tell you this to upset you. I just feel that her actions were not those of someone who dislikes you."

He nodded.

"Are you hungry? I can show you how the kitchen works if you want."

Marrick followed Naya into the room with the cold box and the magic flame. He tried to listen to what she was explaining to him, but his mind kept wandering to Sam. That she had been willing to sacrifice herself to help him.

He wasn't sure if he was grateful or angry...maybe both.

She was a confusing female. And if he couldn't fix things with the portal right now, maybe he should figure out why Sam would protect him one moment and fear him the next.

CHAPTER 11

Sam's nerves were jangling. Now that Marrick had left the hospital, she was worried he was going to overdo it. Worse, the extra tests Sabrina had run didn't suggest any potential cure for Marrick.

He might be feeling better because of whatever Lela did with her energy, but how long would it last?

But she wasn't his keeper. And since she wasn't working, she needed to find something to do. She returned to Irina's house and wasn't surprised to find her in the kitchen making a platter of sandwiches.

"Do I want to know what army you're feeding now?" Sam asked.

Irina chuckled. "Sergei and Lela are moving into their new home today. So we're taking over sandwiches for them, and the movers, and the rest of the family who will show up uninvited to help. Actually, Sergei and Lela are moving out of the apartment you'll be moving into." Irina piled turkey and Swiss on some bread. "It's working out perfectly."

"Do you need any help?" Sam asked.

"Why don't you finish chopping the veggies there on the counter so we can add them to the pasta salad I'm making to eat with the sandwiches."

Sam gaped at the enormous pile of veggies. "How much pasta salad are we making?"

Irina laughed. "Don't ask."

Sam washed her hands and got to work, finding the monotony of chopping the veggies therapeutic.

"Sam? Did you hear what I said?" Irina asked.

"I'm sorry, I zoned out."

"I was asking how Marrick's doing."

"He's okay for now. Boris came to the hospital, and Marrick left with him."

"Boris will watch out for him. And the team will figure out how to open the portal again," Irina said.

Sam hoped so. "I don't understand how this whole portal thing even works."

Irina separated romaine lettuce leaves and started putting them on the sandwiches before answering Sam. "The portal used to be open between earth and the realm. When the war happened and the five clans were sent to the realm, the portal was locked. Now it's used by the guards to travel to earth and the in-between."

"What is the in-between?" Sam asked.

"It's the home for the guards, a place between the realm and earth. All the guards have the ability to move to the realm from the in-between, but only a few guards can open a portal to earth. Originally it was only Naya and Marrick, but now that Naya lives on earth, Krell, Marrick's second in charge, also has the ability."

"So Marrick is the leader?" Sam asked.

"Yes."

Sam dropped the veggies into a large bowl. "So how are they given the ability to open the portal to earth?"

"They have a portal device implanted in their side."

Sam wiped her hands on a towel. "Do we know how it works? Is it biological, mechanical, magical?"

"I don't know for sure. It might be a combination of all three. What are you thinking, Sam?" Irina asked.

"I'm thinking that if we don't know how it works, how will we know how to fix it?"

Irina tilted her head to the side and looked at Sam for a moment. Had she said too much? But then Irina nodded.

"You have a point. I think you need to let Aleksei and Boris know what you're thinking. They might have started down this path, but if not, then let's lead them down it."

Sam blinked. She didn't know if questioning what Boris and Aleksei were doing was the smartest thing to do. She had only been in the compound for a few days, and she wasn't sure if anyone would welcome her opinion.

"I don't know."

Irina huffed at her. "Don't go shy on me now, Sam. I'm going to tell Boris and Aleksei to meet us at Sergei and Lela's house for lunch. You can bring it up then. Now, get back to chopping. There are still a lot of vegetables sitting on the counter."

"Yes, ma'am," Sam said.

An hour later they were packing paper plates, condiments, sandwiches, brownies, and the biggest bowl of pasta salad Sam had ever seen, into a sedan that appeared when they opened the front door, driven by Grigori.

He drove them a few streets over to a new house with a moving truck parked in front. Irina bustled out of the car and waved at the two large males who were unloading furniture.

"Lunch is here, Anton and Dmitry. When you can take a break, come inside."

Why wasn't Sam surprised to learn Irina knew the movers? She lugged the heavy bowl into the house, wondering if someone could get a hernia from carrying pasta salad.

Sergei grabbed the bowl with a grunt and set it on the kitchen counter. He smirked at Lela, who was putting dishes away in the cupboards. "You owe me twenty bucks. I told you Grandmother would be here with food."

"I don't know what I was thinking," Lela said.

Grigori carried in the tray of sandwiches and set them on the counter as well, and Irina arrived right behind him with the dessert.

"I made your favorite, Lela. Salted caramel brownies."

"Yum! Thank you, Irina."

"I'm expecting your father and brothers to be here shortly."

Sergei nodded. "Me too. I'll put them to work if I can."

Irina patted Sergei's arm. "You tell me what you need them to do, and I'll put them to work."

Sergei laughed. "I have no doubt. How's Marrick doing?"

"He's out of the hospital and staying with Boris," Irina said.

"Good. Hopefully they'll have some news about what's going on."

A few minutes later Aleksei, Callie, and Misha arrived, with Misha making a beeline for the pasta salad.

Since Misha was busy chewing, Aleksei brought them up to speed with what they knew so far. Which wasn't much, in Sam's opinion, but what did she know about running an investigation—or realm demons, or portals for that matter?

But Irina apparently thought Sam knew something, since she told Aleksei he needed to talk to her. Before he could make his way to her, Boris, Naya, and Marrick arrived.

Marrick wasn't wearing his uniform. Instead, he had on a blue Henley shirt and a pair of jeans that looked a little too good on him. Sam shut down the thought immediately. She couldn't forget what clan he came from.

"Even better," Irina said. "Naya and Marrick should be able to answer your questions."

Crap. Now everyone was looking at her, including Marrick.

"What question?" Naya asked.

"Well, Aleksei explained what you're doing to figure out who's blocking the portal, but I think we should also be trying to figure out *how* they're blocking the portal. We know this isn't just something that was done to Marrick, since Naya can't open the portal either." Sam looked around the kitchen at the circle of faces. "And it's not just happening on earth, since Aleksei says one of the portal guards in the realm couldn't open the portal either. So I guess that's my long-winded lead-in to ask...how does the portal work?"

Naya and Marrick exchanged a look before Naya responded. "The portal is a link between earth and the realm. It reminds me of a tube connecting two realities."

"Wouldn't the reality be a similar version of earth with different versions of ourselves on it?"

Everyone stared at her for a moment.

Heat rushed to her face. "Sorry. I've watched too many sci-fi shows."

Misha nodded. "You're talking about parallel universes. The realm is really a disparate reality. I sometimes wonder if the portal is some sort of wormhole connecting us to another place millions of miles away."

"So we don't know for sure."

Boris shook his head. "Most of us weren't alive when the portal was created."

Irina spoke up. "I was a child, so I don't remember much. But I think the realm was discovered by the Kelmar."

"But they were sent to the realm. So it was used against them?" Sam asked.

Irina placed her hand on Lela's arm. "Can you tell us anything about your clan, Lela?"

"Stories were passed down by Kelmar, generation after generation. It's been said that the Abstatholm were the ones who discovered the realm, and their ability was captured by the earther clans and used as a weapon."

"Abstatholm?" Sam asked.

"Abstatholm are Kelmar who have the ability to travel through space," Marrick said.

Sam gaped at Lela.

"I can't do it. Only a very small percentage of Kelmar are born Abstatholm. I only know of a couple living right now."

"Are any on earth we can talk to?" Aleksei asked.

"No. Except Joran." Lela looked over at Callie.

Misha put his arm around his mate's shoulders.

Aleksei frowned. "Not an option."

Based on the tight looks on everyone's faces, Joran must be bad news. Sam wasn't going to push her luck by asking about it. "What do we know about the portal devices?"

"Each guard is implanted with a device that allows them to travel between the realm and the in-between. Three of us can also travel to earth," Marrick said.

"Can we get one of the devices to look at?" Sam asked.

Naya shook her head. "The smaller devices are located in the in-between. The devices Marrick, Krell, and I wear are controlled."

"For obvious reasons, the devices were limited," Boris said. "The twelve clan leaders on earth each have one, and I gave the one I had to Naya when her device was destroyed."

"So we go to one of the leaders sympathetic to our cause and see if they'll let us borrow it for testing," Misha said.

Boris nodded. "After the call with the Council tonight, Aleksei and I will talk with one of them and try to convince them. But we need to figure out who's the best one to approach."

"And once we have a device, we can have Sabrina look at it," Aleksei said. He turned to Sam. "Good thinking."

Sam felt her face heat and shrugged. "I just thought if we know how it works—"

"We can figure out how they stopped it," Marrick finished her thought.

"Right," Sam said.

Marrick gazed at her for a drawn-out moment. And she looked back at him. What was it about those blue-violet eyes?

Again, so not going there. She wanted to help him get better, that's all.

That was all it could ever be.

CHAPTER 12

Sam was tired, but it was a good tired. After lunch they stayed for a few hours helping unpack and set up the house.

With all the hands, including the movers (who Sam wasn't surprised to find out were related to the family), they set up the majority of the house—to the delight of Lela and Sergei. Even Boris took off his very expensive suit jacket, rolled up his sleeves, and helped move some furniture.

Finally the family began to trickle away. Naya and Aleksei went to pick up Kara at daycare and spend some time with her before the Council call later.

Callie and Misha left to pick up the twins from school, and Marrick and Boris left as well.

Irina kissed both Lela and Sergei on the cheek before declaring she was ready to head for home.

Sergei and Lela insisted that they take the remaining pasta salad home, so Sam grabbed the bowl and lugged it outside.

Grigori suddenly appeared from nowhere, stopping the car at the curb in front of the house. Irina shook her head, and she and Sam climbed into the car.

"We could have walked home, Grigori."

"Of course you could, Irina."

"I walk all over this compound all the time."

"Of course you do."

Irina sighed. "I can't even have an argument with him, he's so agreeable."

"Well, I for one am glad he showed up. Even though some of this pasta's been eaten, it still weighs a ton," Sam announced.

When he pulled the car up to the house, Grigori insisted on carrying the pasta salad into the house, much to Sam's embarrassment.

And of course Irina then insisted on packing a small container of pasta salad for Grigori before he left.

Apparently it was Irina's mission in life to feed the entire clan.

Irina shooed her out of the kitchen when Sam tried to help her clean up. She headed to the bedroom, kicked off her shoes, and dropped onto the twin bed.

Being around Irina and her happy family made Sam miss her mother. She closed the door and sat down on the bed again with the burner phone.

"Hi, Sam."

"Mom."

"Is something wrong?"

"No. Just felt like talking. I'm chilling out for a few minutes. Irina is like that drum-pounding pink bunny who never slows down," Sam said before flopping back onto the bed.

Gwen laughed. "She sounds fun."

"It's so good to hear you laugh, Mom."

"If feels good to laugh. You sound pretty happy yourself."

"I'm cautiously optimistic."

"Coming from you, that's a ringing endorsement."

Sam sighed. "Fun-ny."

"So tell me what you did that you need to chill out?"

Sam filled her mom in on helping with the move and what the team had found out so far about the issues with the portal.

"You did a good thing today," Gwen said.

"What thing?" Sam asked.

"Speaking up about the portal and the portal device."

"It was just my medical training kicking in. You can't heal without knowing how a body works. I was afraid I shouldn't have spoken up."

"Well, it sounds like they were all glad you did. They took your suggestions seriously."

"Boris has been a bit of a surprise," Sam said.

"How so?"

"We didn't exactly get off on the right foot."

"You mean when you crashed their meeting and told him off?"

Sam sat up. "He was being a condescending ass."

Gwen chuckled. "And you didn't let him get away with it. It sounds like Marrick must be feeling better, if he helped with the move today.

Sam couldn't stifle her frown. "He shouldn't have been doing anything. He's still recuperating."

"Were you able to figure anything out from the additional tests?"

"No. Sabrina has never seen anything like this."

"Maybe he'll get better on his own?"

"That's what Sabrina hopes—the longer he stays here, the more his cells will revert to normal."

"What do you think?"

Leave it to her mother to know she was worried.

"I hope Sabrina's right, but my gut's telling me he needs to go through the portal."

"They'll figure it out with your help," Gwen said.

Sam sighed and shook her head. "You're my biggest cheerleader, Mom."

"You're an amazing female. How could I not be?"

Gwen hesitated for a moment and Sam's alarms started ringing.

"Marrick seems like an honorable male."

And there it was. "Possibly. But he's still a Pavel."

Gwen sighed. "Sam, I did you a disservice."

"What are you talking about?"

"I taught you to fear an entire clan of demons. I'm sorry, because it isn't fair to you or to the Pavel."

Sam gripped the phone tighter. "Are you kidding me? We've spent the past one hundred and fifty years running from them. You didn't do them a disservice! Their actions speak loud and clear."

"Yes. But I don't think they're all bad. And remember, Marrick wasn't raised on earth. He lives a very simple life—in a hut, for goodness' sake. His parents volunteered to watch over the realm, and he followed their selfless path."

"Why are you telling me all this?"

"Because I listen to what you aren't saying. There's a spark there, Sam. And I don't want you to not explore this possibility because of a prejudice I helped instill in you."

Sam's eyes widened. "Mom, I just got here. I'm not in any position for a relationship. Hell, I don't even know if I'm going to stay. Why would I get close to the others when I have to be ready to move at a moment's notice?"

Gwen sighed. "I think this place is different. That this clan would accept you. Just be open, Sam. That's all I ask."

Sam hesitated. "I've got to get going."

"Love you."

"Love you too, Mom."

She wasn't sure what had gotten into her mother lately. Why was she pushing for Sam to fit into this clan? It made her nervous. Her mother was up to something.

A few minutes later Sam found Irina in the kitchen putting pasta salad into smaller containers. Many, many smaller containers. Sam gaped at the stack of containers on the table.

"Hello, dear. I could use your help."

"Of course."

"This pasta salad is not going to fit in my refrigerator. I was going to pack these into some bags to take to the community center kitchen. There's a pantry to the right of the kitchen with shelves of food and a refrigerator with a flower painted on the front. That's the sharing pantry."

Sam gaped at her again. "Sharing pantry?"

"Yes. Anyone in the compound can share food there. You can add and take food as needed."

"Your clan keeps surprising me."

"It's about caring for others. If we all thought that way, the earth and the realm would be much better places."

"I'll take them for you."

"Thank you."

They put the containers into two handled bags, and Sam struggled a bit when she picked them up. Luckily she didn't have far to go.

Sam made it to the community kitchen and found the pantry Irina was talking about. Shelves full of nonperishable items greeted her, as did a large refrigerator with a jaunty-looking sunflower painted on the front.

She stashed the pasta containers in the refrigerator and headed back down the hall.

Voices echoed, and she stopped outside the conference room and peeked inside. She really needed to get out of the habit of eavesdropping, but she couldn't help herself, especially when she saw who was in the room. Boris, Aleksei, and Kyle were sitting in front of a computer facing a large screen on the wall with different types of demons on the screen and their names and clan name listed under their faces.

Naya, Marrick, Misha, and the BSR team stood to the side, out of the laptop camera's view.

Boris welcomed each leader. One square with the name *Josiah Akers, Pavel* at the bottom remained black.

"Josiah, are you there?" Boris asked.

"Yes. The damn camera isn't working on the computer. I'll keep working on it. Do you remember the good old days, Boris? None of this online crap."

Boris chuckled. "Yes."

"Let's plan a golf outing when I'm back in town. It's been a long time."

Sam's nerves stood at attention. But what set them off?

"Of course," Boris said. "Since you can hear us, I'm going to get this meeting started. The main purpose of this meeting is to let you know we have an issue with the portal."

"What type of incident?" the clan leader in the upper right-hand corner asked.

"Aleksei?" Boris said.

Aleksei explained the portal was temporarily blocked. He didn't use Marrick's name or tell them he'd been hurt.

All the leaders started talking at once.

Boris held up his hands. "One at a time, please."

"Why did you wait a day to tell us?" the Haltrap leader said.

"My priority was to ensure the safety of my clan. Plus, I wanted to determine if this was simply a glitch, so I waited to find out if we could reactivate it."

"And obviously it didn't work," Josiah said. "This immigration has been a disaster from the beginning. We can't trust the realm demons."

Kyle sat bolt upright, frowning. "I don't need to remind you that part of this disaster you're talking about was due to earth demons trying to stop the immigration in the beginning."

"What have you found out so far?" Amelia, the Dalmot clan leader, asked.

Aleksei spoke up. "We are trying to determine who or what is blocking the portal. We'll keep you apprised when we know more. The investigation just started."

"If we can't get the portal working again, that would solve the problem, now wouldn't it?" Akers said.

"Seriously?" Kyle blurted.

"I'm only voicing what others are too scared to say."

Boris laid his hand on Kyle's arm when it looked like she was ready to leap through the computer and rain a world of hurt down on the Pavel leader. And here Sam's mother had told Sam to give Pavel a chance, and then their leader showed what an evil male in power was capable of.

"Well, you're not in charge of this immigration," Kyle said.

"Maybe it's time for a change in leadership," Akers responded.

Sam's stomach twisted at his words. She jerked back from the door and hit the wall.

Using the wall to hold her up, she stumbled down the hall and out the door. Why was she having trouble breathing? She didn't understand why Akers's sneering comments felt like they were choking her.

Maybe it was years of hiding away. And she had been looking at all the demon leaders. Any one of them would come after her if they knew who she was. Who her mother was—especially Josiah Akers.

And from what Sam had just witnessed, he would not show them any mercy.

CHAPTER 13

Marrick stood to one side of the room and watched the talking faces on the wall. Naya had tried to explain to him what would happen before the meeting, but he still couldn't believe it.

As he listened to the leaders asking their questions, he realized the magic of the faces on the wall didn't mean the demons themselves were magical. Some were as close-minded as the realm demons had first been about the immigration.

The Pavel leader especially was an embarrassment to Marrick. How could someone like this lead his clan? But then Marrick really wasn't part of the clan, was he?

Frantic emotions slammed into him. He flinched at the strength of them as he looked around the room. No one inside the room was projecting that kind of emotion. But it was there and visceral...confusion and terror so thick it hurt to breathe.

His first instinct was to push the emotions away, but instead he concentrated. Whoever was projecting them was in the hallway.

Is something wrong? Naya asked telepathically.

I need to go outside.

He edged along the wall slowly so he wouldn't interrupt the meeting, and stepped into the hall.

The emotions clung to the air like a wet blanket, but whoever had been feeling them was gone.

He jogged down the hall and opened the side door. Looking around outside, he didn't see anyone at first. But someone was pacing along the lake at the back of the center.

Sam.

He took off toward her, forcing himself to walk instead of running so he wouldn't scare her, especially if she was the one who had been in the center.

"Sam."

She turned toward him. He was several steps away from her, but he could still feel the remnants of the terror surrounding her.

Marrick closed the distance between them and placed his hands on her arms. "Are you okay?"

Sam looked down at his hands, and he dropped them away from her.

She cleared her throat. "I'm fine."

She was clearly lying. He looked at the lake for a moment. Did he want to share his empathic abilities with her? He didn't tell others because they would start treating him differently, and almost inevitably back away from him both physically and emotionally.

Sam didn't trust him now as it was.

"I was in the community center in the meeting with the clan leaders, and I saw someone outside the door."

She narrowed her eyes and backed up.

"I went out into the hall, and the person had already run away. And I came outside and saw you."

She crossed her arms. "And you thought I was in the hall?"

"You have eavesdropped in the past."

"I'm never going to live that down. It wasn't me."

She was a horrible liar, but her closed-off expression told him if he pushed her, she would run.

"Well, someone was there. Hopefully they didn't need some sort of help."

Sam looked away. "Why would you want to help a stranger?"

"Why wouldn't I?"

Sam's eyes widened. "You keep surprising me."

And he could say the same. But he didn't. Because only moments ago she'd been scared and confused, and now she was hiding her feelings from him. He wanted to help her. But he didn't understand this world or her well enough to know what to do.

"Can I walk with you to Irina's?"

She hesitated for a moment before nodding, and they started off along the side of the lake.

He would spend time with her so she could see he wasn't someone to be afraid of. He got the impression that she didn't allow many to get close to her. Or let them see her true feelings, even though her expressive face did give some clues to her innermost thoughts. Expressive and beautiful.

He almost stumbled. Where had that come from? Time to redirect his wayward thoughts. "Do you like your new home?"

"So far. It's definitely not boring around here."

"Very true. Have you lived many places?"

He could feel her nervousness swell again.

"Why do you ask?"

"I'm curious if you have seen much of earth. I have lived in the in-between my whole life. I can't imagine seeing all this world and what it has to offer. Just being in this compound is remarkable."

She smiled. "I can imagine. I've lived many places over the years."

"You don't miss your clan?"

Sam shook her head. "I've never experienced the kind of support this clan gives each other. They're special."

"I'm glad Naya found her place here."

He could feel Sam's eyes on him, so he turned her way. "What?"

"You seem close to Naya. It's none of my business, but were you involved with her in the past?"

"No. We're friends...more like siblings, really. When she fought her feelings for Aleksei, I had to work hard to get her to tell him the truth."

"It must have worked."

"Yes, the two stubborn goats finally admitted they loved each other."

Sam smiled, shaking her head. "I think you mean stubborn mules."

He was happy to see her smile. More than he should be. "They are both animals, right?"

"Yes."

"Are mules more stubborn than goats?" he asked.

Sam shrugged. "I guess so. Although I have heard goats pretty much do what they want, too, so maybe it's a tie. Naya and Aleksei make an interesting couple."

"Yes. And finding out they were with child was a wonderful surprise for both of them."

Sam stopped walking. "What do you mean? How could having the baby be a surprise when demons know when they're in cycle."

"Not the females traveling back and forth to the realm. Sabrina believes cycles can change due to the fluctuating time."

Sam shook her head. "Now you have to explain what you mean."

"A week's time on earth is like a month in the realm."

"Wow. That's amazing. So when Aleksei talks about bringing demons here in two weeks, it really means two months for those waiting in the realm."

"Correct." Marrick nodded. "You are curious. Maybe that's what makes you such a good nurse."

Pink stained her cheeks. "Well, I hope we can find a way to open the portal again."

Marrick stopped in front of Irina's house. "We'll figure it out. There's no other option, and I have learned that this clan is made up of a bunch of stubborn mules or goats."

And there was the smile he liked so much.

"How are you feeling, by the way?"

"Fine." Very tired, but she didn't need to know that.

She narrowed her eyes at him.

"Do you not believe me?"

"I believe you will work through pain to do your job. It's part of the warrior code, right?"

"You think I'm a warrior?"

"Aren't you?" Sam sighed. "Until you can travel back through the portal and restore your cells, you really do need to take it easy, Marrick."

"Which is why I'm working with the clan to figure this out."

Sam scowled up at him. Frustration pulsed from her. "If you don't take care of yourself, I will have Dr. Miller pull rank and sideline you."

"Sideline?"

"She will put you on bed rest."

He shook his head. "Oh, no. Naya was on bed rest while she was with child. I am not staying in bed."

Sam crossed her arms. "Then you need to take it easy."

He crossed his own arms. "You are very bossy."

"You just told me I'm a good nurse, so you can't take it back just because you don't like what I'm telling you."

She rested her hand on his arm, and he felt it like a brand.

"Promise me you'll take care of yourself. You're not going to be able to help anyone if you don't rest. You need to come to the hospital tomorrow to have Sabrina check you over."

"Bossy."

She shrugged. "You already said that. It won't deter me."

"Stubborn."

She grinned up at him, and his breath hitched. "If your next words include goat or mule, you are in big trouble."

He couldn't help but smile. "I'll see you tomorrow, Sam."

She opened Irina's door and stepped inside, turning around at the last moment. "See that you do," she said before she shut the door.

Marrick stared at the closed door. Sam was such a confusing female. He had never met anyone like her.

She was forthright and caring in one breath and vulnerable the next. He was fascinated by her. For now he would have to wait to unwrap the layers she had built around herself. First, he needed to figure out how to fix the portal and hopefully heal himself in the process. Then he would explore his fascination with this feisty nurse.

CHAPTER 14

Sam hurried down the hospital corridor to the front desk. She was working intake. The hospital served a dual purpose, also providing clinic visits and urgent care in addition to hospital stays. Her job today was to greet the clinic patients and handle any urgent care arrivals.

Which hopefully would keep her busy and her mind from spending too much time on Marrick. He hadn't come to see Sabrina for a checkup yet, even after Sam practically threatened him last night.

She wasn't sure if Marrick believed last night's lie about not being in the community center. Her mother always told her to avoid lying since she wasn't good at it. Which makes things difficult when you're on the run. Normally she tried to stick as close as she could to some version of the truth, except last night. She wasn't sure why she didn't just admit she'd been standing outside the room, but her emotions had been so scrambled.

And now she was thinking about Marrick again. What happened to keeping busy?

When she got back to the front desk, Corinne said, "You already took the last patient back. Once he's done, it'll be time for a lunch break before our next patient at one."

Sam flipped the chart cover open. "No urgent care patients?"

"Just the earache you took care of earlier."

Sam nodded. She didn't want anyone to be ill, but it made for a slow day if no one came into urgent care.

The doors swished open and Marrick strode into the reception area, but he wasn't alone. The twins, Matty and Luke, were each perched on one hip, supported by his arms. Luke was crying and Matty's eyes were wide as he looked around.

"What's going on, guys?" Sam asked.

"Luke fell out of a tree," Marrick said.

Alarm bells sounded in Sam's head as she began to think about all the injuries that could result from a fall.

"How far did he fall?" Sam asked.

"Marrick caught him like Superman!" Matty blurted.

"So he didn't hit the ground?"

"No, he fell a few feet before I caught him, but the branches scraped his arm on the way down."

Sam nodded. "Corinne, would you pull the boys' charts and look up Callie's number and call her?"

"No need. I have her number memorized."

I bet she does. "Okay, let's go check your arm, Luke."

Sam led them down the hall into an exam room, where Marrick set Luke on the exam table and Matty on the chair against the wall.

"Okay, let's hear what happened," Sam said as she rolled a tray with supplies over to the table.

She rested her hand on Luke's shoulder, and after a moment he hiccuped and stopped crying.

Luke and Matty exchanged looks, and Sam glanced between them as she pulled on gloves. "Ah, ah, ah. Don't think about changing the story. What happened?"

The boys' eyes widened before Matty sighed. "I bet Luke he couldn't climb the tree like Misha the cat did."

Marrick crossed his arms. "The same Misha we had to rescue out of the tree the other day?"

Matty looked down at his shoes as he kicked his feet. "Yeah, we didn't think about that."

Sam picked up a penlight. "I'm going to look into your eyes, Luke." She worked quickly, and was happy to see his pupils respond normally.

"Did you hit your head when you fell?"

"No. Just my arm."

Sam felt along his arm, checking for breaks. "Does this hurt?"

"Just the scratch."

The bottom of Luke's sleeve was torn, so she cut the rest of the sleeve off and took a look at his arm.

"It's a hard scrape, but I don't think you'll need stiches. I'm going to clean it up."

Sam wiped off the scrape and then leaned in to look for chunks of wood or splinters that might have been embedded in the wound.

"Where were you two supposed to be?" Sam asked.

"What do you mean?" Matty and Luke said at the same time.

"I don't think you were supposed to be climbing trees in the middle of the day."

Luke sighed. "School finished early. We were going to BB's."

"Irina's house is down the street from the school. How did you end up in a tree?"

"It was on the way to her house," Matty said, as if that made perfect sense.

Marrick looked at her, and she shook her head slightly before working on Luke's arm again.

The intercom buzzed.

"Yes, Corinne."

"I wasn't able to get through to Callie, so I called Misha. He's on his way."

"Thanks. Call Irina and let her know the boys are here. Also, have Dr. Miller stop in when she has a moment," Sam said.

The boys groaned.

"What's wrong?" Sam asked.

"Papa's going to get warts," Luke said.

"What?"

"We heard Momma talking about him with Aunt Naya. She said when he worries, he gets warts."

Marrick's jaw dropped in what could only be horror, and Sam tried her darndest not to laugh, but a small chuckle erupted.

"Did she call him a worrywart?"

"Yes," Matty said.

"That just means he worries a lot. He won't get warts."

"Ohhh," the boys and Marrick said at the same time.

Sam did laugh out loud that time. "You should see the looks on your faces."

The boys giggled and Marrick's eyes danced.

"What's all this laughing about?" Sabrina asked when she walked in.

The boys perked up when they saw her, and they repeated their story while Sabrina looked Luke over before holding her hands above him and using her healing senses.

She patted him on the shoulder. "You'll be fine, but no more scaling trees without permission, okay?"

The boys nodded.

"And your papa worries about you because he loves you," Sabrina added.

The boys grinned. "We are lovable," Matty said.

"Yep," Luke agreed.

Marrick coughed, but Sam was pretty sure he was covering up a laugh.

"Really?" Sabrina said.

"Yep, BB told Papa we're lovable," Matty said.

Luke nodded. "She also said we're precocious. But we don't know what that means."

"It means you are much smarter than seven-year-olds should be," Sabrina said before turning to Sam. "Let's get an antibiotic gel on the scrape and bandage it."

Footsteps pounded toward them and the boys exchanged a look. "Here comes Papa."

A few minutes later, after Misha had hugged the boys until they squeaked, thanked Marrick profusely, and then launched into his lecture while he escorted the boys out of the room, Sabrina turned to Marrick.

"I'm glad you're here. Sam said you were coming in today, so I set aside time to check you over and see how you're doing."

Marrick turned to Sam for a moment. "Did she tell you she threatened me if I didn't come in today?"

Sabrina tilted her head slightly. "Did she?"

Sam wasn't sure what the head tilt meant exactly. Good or bad?

"I hired her because she's a good nurse."

Good, then. Sam let out the breath she'd been holding, pulled the paper down the exam table, and ripped off the used piece.

Marrick stared at what she was doing, looking bemused. She couldn't imagine how this world looked to him.

Sabrina gestured for Marrick to take a seat, and Sam put the blood pressure cuff on his arm and the pulse ox on his finger. Both were high.

Sabrina circled the exam table, stopped in front of Marrick, and held up her hands with her eyes closed, standing still and silent.

Sam found herself holding her breath again.

After a drawn-out moment, Sabrina dropped her hands. "Your energy is still all over the place. How do you feel?"

Marrick hesitated, and before Sam could speak up, Sabrina narrowed her eyes at him. "Truth, please."

"I'm tired."

"And?" Sam prompted.

He glanced at her before facing Sabrina again. "And I don't feel right. Like my skin is too tight."

Sam tried to keep her expression neutral. What were they going to do for him? They hadn't helped him...not really...and she wanted to yell at the Fates.

"Let's take some more blood, and after that there's another test I want to run," Sabrina said. "I'll be right back to get you."

Sam nodded as she turned to the cupboard and pulled out the supplies she needed for a blood draw. When she stepped up to Marrick, he gave her a long look before pulling up his sleeve. She tied the tourniquet and wiped his arm with alcohol.

"You're going to feel a prick," Sam said before inserting the needle and drawing two tubes of blood. She pulled the needle out. "Can you press this on your arm?"

Marrick pressed the gauze to his arm and looked up at her. "We all know this isn't going to help me."

"We don't know that at all. Dr. Miller is a good doctor. She wants to help you."

"I know she's a powerful healer. But some things can't be healed."

A heavy weight settled in Sam's chest. "What do you mean?"

"We need to get the portal fixed."

Sam wrapped the stretch bandage around the gauze on his arm. "And we'll get you through the portal as soon as we can."

"We?"

Sam felt her face warm, so she looked down at the tray and began cleaning up. "Everyone is working hard to get the portal working again."

"I know. It's important to keep the immigration running."

She looked up at him. "And to help you too."

He shook his head. "I am not the priority."

Sam turned to place the tray on the counter. "Could you be any more noble?" she murmured.

"What?"

She faced him. "I said, maybe it's time to make yourself a priority."

His eyebrows rose. "I'm a guard. And as such, we take an oath to protect. And if it means sacrificing ourselves, then so be it."

Sam crossed her arms. "I get it, but things are different now. Your job has changed. Now you're helping the very demons you kept imprisoned come to earth. You'll get to be something other than a guard. Have you thought of that?"

"I haven't let myself think too much about it."

"Why not?" Sam asked.

Marrick paused. "Because we still have demons both in the realm and on earth who oppose this migration. And we still have work to do."

"Which brings us back to opening the portal again."

"Yes. But even if we open the portal—"

Sam interrupted him. "*When* we open the portal."

"*When* we open the portal, we don't know whether it will help me or not."

Sam swallowed down the boulder lodged in her throat. "So let Sabrina run her tests as a backup plan."

"Okay, stubborn one."

Sam shrugged and smiled. "I've been called worse."

Marrick smiled back, and she lost her ability to suck in a deep breath. Had she ever seen him smile before? He definitely needed to do it more often.

Sabrina peeked her head in. "Ready for the test?"

Marrick nodded before following Sabrina out of the room.

Hours later Marrick's words still echoed in Sam's head while she finished her shower and pulled on her pj's before falling into bed.

She sucked in a shaky breath. What if they couldn't help him?

Sam reached for her phone and dialed. "Hi, Mom."

"Hi, honey. What's wrong?"

Her mother was uncanny sometimes. "All I said was 'hi.'"

"That's all you need to say for me to know something's wrong, so spill."

"We haven't been able to open the portal again, which means the immigration can't continue."

"It's only been a few days, right? You'll figure it out, I'm sure."

Sam sighed. "I hope so."

"Your being upset wouldn't be about Marrick, would it?"

"We haven't found a way to help him." Sam swallowed. "I'm scared we're running out of time."

"You'll find a way, I have no doubt. I'm so proud of you."

"For what?"

"For being willing to step up and help. It makes me so happy that you've found a clan to be a part of."

Sam closed her eyes. "It's only temporary."

"It doesn't have to be," her mother responded.

Sam's nerves jumped under her skin. "How can you say that? We never stay anywhere for long. It's how this works."

"It doesn't have to work that way for you."

"We're a team. We'll be back together soon."

Gwen didn't say anything.

Sam sat up. "What aren't you telling me, Mom?"

"Nothing. I just want you to remember you have a choice, Sam."

Sam gripped the phone tightly. "I know I do. And my choice will always be you."

"Let's not worry about the future right now. Just concentrate on helping Marrick and the clan. We'll talk soon."

Sam looked down at her phone. Her mother hung up before Sam could protest.

What the hell was her mom up to?

CHAPTER 15

Marrick entered the conference room to find a circle of people surrounding the table, all staring at the small silver cylinder in the center.

Sam leaned close to it, as if she was trying to see inside the portal device. Sabrina stood across from her with Aleksei and Naya on one side and Boris on the other.

Boris patted Marrick on the back. "Glad you could make it."

"You were able to convince a clan leader to give you a portal device."

Boris nodded. "Yes. Amelia, the Dalmot leader, gave it to us to examine."

"I wasn't expecting it to be so small," Sam said.

Sabrina leaned closer as well and studied it. "It can't be too big, since it's inserted in the traveler's side."

"Can we open it?" Sam asked.

Sabrina shook her head. "I think we need to scan it first. We don't want it to blow up."

Sam backed up. "Blow up?"

"If someone besides the user tries to remove it from their body, the device explodes," Sabrina explained.

"Is it mechanical, biological, or magical?" Sam asked.

"I think it might be all three," Naya said. "When it's embedded, it becomes a part of the traveler. As Sabrina said, the device will destroy itself if it senses someone else trying to take it."

"So there has to be some sort of biological signature it attaches itself to," Sam said.

"Agreed," Sabrina said.

"And magic too," Naya said. "We can travel to another reality, or dimension, or universe. Whatever we want to call it, we can do it. How can there not be magic involved?"

Kyle and Misha walked in.

"What did we miss?" Kyle asked.

"We've all been standing here staring at the portal device," Aleksei said with a smirk.

Kyle shook her head. "It's a good thing we're here, then."

"What news do you have for us, Kyle?" Boris asked.

"Sylvia's heard some rumors on the street that the immigration's been stopped. Jean Luc should be here shortly. He's picking up Galim."

Sam looked confused, so Kyle explained. "Galim is a realm demon who has the ability to recognize different demon energies and realm power. We thought it might be helpful for him to examine the portal device."

The group made room for Misha and Kyle at the table and then they all resumed staring at the device.

A few minutes later Jean Luc and a tall, thin male joined them. Introductions were made, and Galim went over to the table. "Can I touch it?"

"Yes," Boris said.

Galim reached out slowly before pausing his hand over the device. It was as if he was feeling the air around it.

"Galim?" Kyle asked.

"It's as if it has a pulse." His eyes widened. "It reminds me of the red crystal in the realm."

Kyle pulled out a crystal that she was wearing around her neck. "Like my necklace?"

"Yes. But this device is more concentrated, as if it contains the power of the crystal caves in its tiny cylinder."

"Do you think that's what makes it work?"

"Partially."

Naya tapped her fingers on the table. "The Kelmar live in the caves. Do you think being surrounded by this energy contributes to them birthing Abstatholm?"

Galim ran his fingers along the metal. "Possibly. It would make sense. If you are immersed in energy, it finds ways to expend itself."

Marrick's vision blurred, and he blinked to clear it. The room came back into focus, but his breath hitched.

"There's the energy I sensed earlier, before we came into the room," Galim said.

"From the portal device?" Kyle asked.

"No." Galim turned to face Marrick. "It's pulsing from him and to him. I've never felt anything like it."

"What?" Marrick said as his breathing seemed to even out.

"Energy, but not." He frowned. "It's as if two opposing forces are fighting each other."

"It's like his cells are in flux," Sabrina said.

"Yes." Galim stared at Marrick again. "And he's not stable."

"What do you mean?" Sam asked. "Do we need to get him to the hospital?"

Galim tilted his head as he studied Marrick. "His energy is sparking, and I don't know if it will stay contained."

Marrick backed away from the group. "If I'm a danger to this clan, I need to leave."

"And go where?" Sam asked.

"Somewhere away from people."

"That's going to be hard to do in Northeast Ohio," Misha said.

Sabrina moved closer and held up her hands in front of him for a few moments with her eyes closed. When she opened them, Marrick didn't like the serious expression. "Your cells are getting more unstable."

Marrick's heart sped up. "I won't be a threat to this clan."

Kyle spoke up. "There will be no throwing yourself off a cliff! And before you ask, there aren't any cliffs around here, so let's think this through."

"What if we remove his portal device?" Naya asked.

Galim shook his head. "The instability is part of him."

"What about having Marrick go to the bunker?" Aleksei asked.

"That should work," Boris said. "The thick metal walls should protect us." Boris grimaced. "Do the trick."

Marrick wanted to get as much distance as possible from all of them, but he didn't know how to accomplish it without putting others outside the compound at risk. "Take me there now."

"Misha, why don't you take Marrick to the backup bunker?" Boris said. "There's water and some basic supplies there, and we'll bring you some more supplies later. And we'll figure this out, Son."

Marrick looked over at Sam, and their eyes met.

"I'll come check on you later, Marrick," Sabrina said.

Marrick nodded, even though he wanted to tell her to stay away from him. To tell all of them to stay away from him.

Sam wanted to scream as she watched Marrick and Misha leave the room.

"What are we going to do?" she asked of no one in particular.

Kyle turned to Galim. "Can you think of anything that might block the portal devices?"

Galim didn't answer immediately. Instead he picked up the portal device and wrapped his fist around it. "I think, in order to block this device, you would need something with similar powers."

"An Abstatholm?" Boris asked.

"We only know of one on the earth right now," Aleksei said.

"So we should talk to him or her," Sam said.

Everyone else exchanged cryptic looks.

"Misha and Callie aren't here to weigh in on that, and they need to be here before we think about seeing Joran," Naya said.

"Joran is the Abstatholm?" Sam asked.

"Yes," Boris answered. "He also attacked Callie and tried to take the twins to the realm."

Sam's stomach bottomed out. "What! Where is he now?"

"He's been locked away and his powers neutralized," Boris said.

"Or so we hope." Aleksei didn't look completely convinced.

"Agreed," Boris said. "So we contact the prison and make sure Joran is still locked up. And then we talk to Misha and Callie before we confront Joran."

The meeting broke up a few minutes later, and Sam went back to the hospital with Sabrina.

"We have to do something, Sabrina."

"I'm worried about Marrick too."

Sam wasn't going to deny she'd been talking about Marrick and not the portal. "But he's locked in the bunker."

"I doubt Misha locked him in, but I understand what you mean."

Once they entered through the hospital's sliding doors, Sabrina beckoned for Sam to follow her to an exam room, where she took out a portable exam pack and held it out to Sam.

"I was going to check on Marrick, but why don't you do a 'house call' instead, and make sure he's settling into the bunker? I'll check on him again later."

Sam reached for the bag and gripped the handle.

"I know you're new here, but I've been working with this group long enough to know we'll figure this out. We won't stop until we do."

Sam believed her, but would it be in time to help Marrick?

Thirty minutes later, Sam still gripped the bag in one hand as she adjusted the duffel bag on her shoulder containing the clothes Misha had loaned Marrick.

A guard stood outside the bunker entrance, and he nodded to Sam as he heaved open the large metal door with a *clank*.

She took the stairs down to a big room with lots of chairs, and shelving along the far wall.

Marrick got to his feet across the room.

"What are you doing here, Sam?"

"It's good to see you too."

He narrowed his eyes at her. "It's not safe to be near me."

She set the duffel on a chair. "I brought your clothes and toiletries. I'm also here to check you over."

He crossed his arms. Apparently he was in full-on stubborn mode. Mule? Goat? It didn't matter. She could do stubborn with the best of them.

"No arguments. Doctor's orders."

Sam crossed the room since he didn't make any move toward her. She set down her bag and unzipped it, then pulled out her BP cuff.

"You're not going to fight me on this, are you?"

His eyes flared before he held out his arm.

She took his BP—which was still too high—and then his pulse.

"You have the little line between your eyebrows that you get when you're worried," he said.

She looked up at him. "It's called a frown line. And I didn't know I had one."

"Like you're thinking too hard."

"You know, you shouldn't tell females they have wrinkles."

He gaped at her like she'd just told him he had bugs coming out of his ears. She couldn't keep the grin off her face. "I'm teasing you. It's not that bad."

His mouth actually quirked up on one side. "You are bad."

She shrugged. "Guilty, but admit it. You almost smiled."

"Is a smile from me your goal?"

"One of them."

He looked at her...really looked at her...and tingling ran up and down her skin.

Fates! She'd never felt like this before, but then the tingling started stinging and she knew something was wrong.

Marrick's eyes widened. "Run!"

She looked behind her, and the air changed, as if turning into molten liquid. Was it a portal? Marrick tried to push her out of the way, but the force pulled her toward it. She screamed and held onto Marrick's arms as her legs were lifted into the air.

"Sam!"

"Don't let go," Sam gasped as panic made it impossible to breathe.

"Never."

His arms strained and he dug in his heels, but they both were dragged closer. Just as shouts sounded in the stairwell, Marrick pulled her against him and they both were sucked into the energy.

Pressure pushed in around them until she couldn't see or hear anything. The only thing she knew was that Marrick hugged her tight to his body. And she took some comfort from it even as she struggled to suck air into her lungs.

After a few more seconds they were expelled from the portal and landed on their feet on a dusty patch of ground.

She gasped and Marrick pushed her away slightly so he could look her up and down.

"Are you okay, Sam?"

Am I? She blinked before nodding. "You?"

"Yes."

She looked around. In front of them was a forest with blue trees. "Do you see blue trees?"

He stiffened next to her. "Yes."

"The realm has blue trees?"

"No."

She spun around and looked up at him. "If this isn't the realm, then where are we?"

His gaze locked on to her for a moment before he looked around. "I don't know.

That was not what Sam wanted to hear. "You don't know?"

He shook his head while maintaining his vigilance. "Let's not stand out in the open."

He grasped her hand and led her toward the trees and into the forest a few feet and then stopped.

"What are we doing?" she asked.

"I don't know if this place is inhabited or not. Until we finish looking around, let's stay in the shadows."

"Right. Because being in the shadows is so much better than the light of day. This is like a horror movie. They always die in the shadows."

"Horror movie?"

"Never mind. Has this ever happened to you before?"

"No. I have only ever traveled between the realm and earth."

Now what? "Well, now that the portal activated again, maybe it's fixed. Do you want to see if you can activate it?"

"It might not be safe."

"We're standing in a forest of blue trees hiding from possible monsters. I think we should risk it."

He grabbed her hand and closed his eyes for a moment. Nothing happened. She bit her lip and waited quietly.

Finally he opened his eyes. "I can't get the portal to activate."

"Okay. So what do we do now?"

"We check our surroundings and find water, food, and shelter."

Crap. They were in trouble.

"We're on our own for now." He blew out a breath and turned into his demon self.

Sam took a step back before she could stop herself.

He frowned, which made his demon self even more intimidating. "I'll figure out how to get you home, Sam. In the meantime, I think we should stay close in case the portal opens again."

He held out his hand, and she hesitated but finally grasped it, and they walked to the tree line while he kept watch over them.

They settled on a fallen tree and he turned to her. "It may be easier for you to turn to your demon self in the realm. It's more natural here to be demon than on earth."

"I can't remember the last time I turned to my demon form. I don't know if I even remember how." Since she and her mother had hidden most of their lives, spending time in their demon forms would have been a foolish risk.

"I just recently learned how to change to human. I can teach you if you want."

She didn't immediately respond.

"Sam, why are you scared of me?"

"I'm not scared of you," she answered much too quickly.

"Then my demon. Every time I turn, fear pulses from you."

How did he know that?

"I'm empathic. I can feel your fear, and even if I wasn't empathic, I can see it in your face and actions."

"Why didn't you tell me you're empathic?"

He blew out a hard breath. "Because of the way you're looking at me right now. When people know I'm empathic, they behave differently around me. They shut themselves off. Now, why don't you tell me why you're scared of my demon?"

So much for changing the subject. How much to tell him? "Let's just say my family wasn't treated well by the Pavel. I know not all Pavel are the same, here." She tapped her finger next to her temple. "But I can't seem to stop the reaction."

Marrick nodded. "It's instinct. Your body is protecting itself. I understand."

She wished she understood what the deep-seated fear was all about. Why her childhood was littered with nightmares of blurred purple faces and angry voices. Her mother had been her only calm in the storm during her childhood.

Sam cringed. Crap. Her mom.

She'd be frantic if she couldn't get a hold of Sam. Depending on how much time had passed on earth, she might have already missed their daily call. She wasn't sure what her mom would do when she couldn't reach her, but whatever it was, it wouldn't be good.

CHAPTER 16

Gwen took a calming breath as she walked away from the front gate of the Shamat compound. The guard she'd just spoken to was back in the building, but she was sure she was still being watched.

When she'd arrived in Cleveland yesterday, she tried to contact the compound to set up a meeting with the clan leader. The same leader whose meeting Sam burst into and told him off. But she'd gotten the runaround. She spoke to some assistant who said Boris wasn't available for a meeting in the foreseeable future. Really?

Over the decades of being on the run, she'd learned to be patient and to check things out before she simply ran headfirst into trouble. So she'd scoped out the compound last night.

But when Sam missed her third call in, Gwen decided to go to the compound and try a face-to-face approach.

It was a huge risk, but Gwen would do anything for her daughter. Anything.

But no matter what she tried, she couldn't get the guard to let her see the clan leader—or anyone else, for that matter.

Which set her alarm bells off. Something wasn't right, and Sam was caught in the middle of it. And Gwen was the one who'd sent her daughter here.

So it was time to take the gloves off and do what she had to do. Gwen climbed back into the car and drove away with every appearance of calm, even though her heart was thumping a staccato beat.

She parked the rental car behind a group of trees, tucking it away from prying eyes.

Getting out of the car, she pulled off her respectable jacket. The tank she had on underneath would be easier to move around in. Next she kicked off the black pumps and pulled on her running shoes; then Gwen calmly braided her hair to get it out of the way.

Heading through the trees, she stopped at the tall metal fence surrounding the compound. Time to pay the Shamat clan a visit.

Gwen grabbed the cast-iron bars and pulled herself up several feet until she hovered at the top. Being on the run didn't mean cowering in the corner. She'd learned how to defend herself and Sam, which demanded she stay in top shape.

Swinging over the top of the fence, she then slid down the other side. Gwen figured she had a minute or less before a guard showed up. Even though surveillance equipment wasn't visible, there had to be cameras somewhere.

She ran away from the fence, heading toward what she hoped was the center of the compound, and when a shout sounded behind her, her feet and heart picked up the pace.

An alarm pierced the air.

Running headfirst into danger went against every instinct she had. But when it came to Sam's safety, instincts be damned.

Boris paced his office. Marrick and Sam had been pulled into the portal three days ago, and still nothing. As soon as it happened, he'd directed his clan to the bunkers, not sure if they were under attack. After they confirmed that only Marrick and Sam were gone, he lowered the alert level, but encouraged his clan to stay in their homes if possible.

Everyone had been working nonstop since then, trying to figure out what the hell had happened. Naya couldn't communicate with Marrick, but she had reached out to the other portal guards and they confirmed that Marrick and Sam weren't in the realm.

Which had everyone worried.

And even though the portal had pulled Marrick and Sam into it, since then no one had been able to activate it.

Where the hell could they be? He couldn't believe the worst. He refused, and so did everyone else. They needed to find them and fix the portal.

This was his clan, his responsibility. And Sam might have been there for only a few days, but she was his responsibility as well.

The compound alarm rang out.

Damn, what now? Boris jogged around his desk and threw open his office door. A guard ran up to him.

"What is it, Nick?"

"Compound breach."

"Do we have eyes on them?"

"Yes. They're engaging now." Nick pressed his fingers to his earpiece, listening. "They have the threat contained."

"How many?"

"One demon."

"I want to interrogate him," Boris said.

"Sir."

"No arguments, Nick. I want to know why the hell he breached our compound."

Boris headed across the compound with Nick alongside him and entered the nondescript building they used as a containment center. The door opened again behind him, and he turned to see Aleksei and Naya walk in.

Another compound guard joined them, sporting a red mark along his jaw that would definitely turn into a bruise.

"Thomas. I take it he put up a fight. Is everyone okay?"

"Yes, sir."

"I want to talk to the prisoner."

They went to the interrogation room to look at the monitor, and Boris blinked...and then blinked again. A petite woman who was dressed like she'd been out for a simple jog sat there quietly. She had long blond hair pulled back from an angular face, but he couldn't make out the color of her eyes since she was looking down. In human years she appeared to be in her late thirties, early forties, which could mean a range of several centuries in demon years.

Aleksei glanced back at Thomas.

"It was just a lucky shot," the guard blurted.

Naya's eyebrow went up, and Boris knew from experience it was not a good sign. "Are you claiming a female can't beat you?" she demanded. "I would be happy to spar with you at a later date."

Thomas very wisely shook his head. "Not what I meant. I just wasn't expecting her to attack."

"What do we know about her?" Aleksei asked.

"No identification, and so far she's refused to answer any of our questions. But she came to the front gate a short time ago asking to see Boris or Irina. She said something about a scheduled meeting, but since you didn't have anything on the schedule, and we've been on lockdown, the guard on duty turned her away."

Boris blew out a breath. "I'm going in to speak to her."

Naya's eyes danced. "I think this is going to get interesting. Do you want me in there to protect you?"

He shook his head at his daughter-in-law before walking down the hall. Nick opened the door for him, and he stepped inside.

Green eyes looked up at him. Emerald green, now that they were face-to-face and he was close enough to see the color. "Based on your fancy suit, I assume you're someone in charge?"

He nodded. "I'm Boris Chesnokov, the Shamat clan leader."

"Finally. You're a hard male to talk to."

"So you felt the need to break into my compound?"

She shrugged. "It got you here."

"There are easier ways to see me. I understand you came to the gate earlier."

"I was turned away. I almost insisted on seeing you, but your guard seemed ready to call the cops. And I figured once I was inside the compound, I had a better chance."

"The moment you came over the fence, we were alerted to your presence."

"I know. If I didn't want to be caught, I wouldn't have been."

Fascinating. "Then why fight my guard?"

"To show how serious I am."

He crossed his arms. "Why don't we stop playing games and you tell me who you are and what you want."

"My name is Gwen and I want to know where my daughter is."

Boris hadn't known what to expect, but it wasn't that. "Who's your daughter?"

"Samantha Taylor. She just moved here to work as a nurse."

Russian expletives flooded Boris's thoughts as he tried to school his expression.

Her eyes narrowed at him. He hadn't covered it up as well as he'd hoped.

"Is she okay?"

Time to deflect. "Sam told us she doesn't have any family."

"Well, she does. Me. Where is my daughter?"

He hesitated while he really looked at her. Even though Gwen had blond hair and Sam brown, they had the same eye shape and small, upturned nose. They were definitely related.

"If you don't know, let me talk to Irina or Marrick."

Her demand caught him off guard. "How do you know about Marrick?"

Her face remained calm, although her hands were clenched. "Sam told me Marrick is a realm guard who's stuck here right now because there's been a malfunction with the portal. She's been taking care of him."

Voices in the hall interrupted before he could say more. The door opened and his mother barged in. Why wasn't he surprised?

"I understand someone wants to see me?"

Gwen looked over at her. "Irina?"

"Yes, dear."

"Where is my daughter, Sam? I can't reach her."

Irina looked over at him. "Tell her, Boris."

He had already decided to tell her, but something about her had his alarm bells going off. "The portal opened, and Sam and Marrick were pulled into it."

Gwen blinked. "Sam's in the realm?"

"No. We've communicated with the realm, and they're not there. We think they were pulled to another reality."

She stood. "You think?"

"Yes. It doesn't make sense that earth and the realm would be the only realities out there. Recently we've been sensing power surges along the portal, and we suspect they're being moved among these realities. We hope it's Marrick trying to get them either back here or to the realm."

Gwen looked between Boris and Irina. "Did this Marrick take Sam?"

Irina stood next to Boris. "No. Marrick is an honorable male. He didn't take her. He'll protect her with his life."

Gwen's eyes tightened on Boris. "So what are you doing, Boris Chesnokov, mighty Shamat clan leader, to get my daughter back?"

This female had no fear. "We're working on it."

"I'm going to help."

He felt his eyebrows rise before he could school his expression. Not *can I help*, but *I'm going to help*. "Are you?"

"Yes. My daughter is in danger. I need to be a part of it. And if you're worried, I'll promise to behave and not punch any more of your guards."

Irina chuckled beside him, and even though he couldn't hear Naya in the observation room, he was sure she was laughing too.

"I'll hold you to that, Gwen."

He wasn't sure he could trust her, but he understood a parent's need to do anything for their family. If Gwen was telling him the truth, she deserved to help bring Sam home safely.

CHAPTER 17

Marrick looked out over the valley as a warm breeze rippled the purple grasses. They had jumped again, for the third time since they first were sucked into the portal to the land with the blue trees.

He didn't care what happened to him, but he needed to get Sam home again. She was sitting on the rock behind him next to their cooking fire. He didn't want her to stray out of reach in case they jumped again.

The idea of her being stuck alone in a strange world tore at his gut like a stab wound. If he lost her, how would he find her again, when he had no way of knowing where they were to begin with?

Not that she was helpless.

Far from it. When she'd gathered kindling and started the fire the first night, he gaped at her. Not because he believed she wasn't capable. Working with Naya had shown him females' true strength. But with everything earth had to offer, he didn't think many of those who lived there truly had to work hard to take care of the day-to-day. Sam had actually laughed at him and proceeded to tell him earth didn't always have all the comforts they had now. She'd learned as a child how to build fires and cook what they were able to gather and hunt.

But he was still worried about her. What if someone or something attacked them? He still needed to deliver her safely back to earth. And he felt the time ticking away. He hadn't told her the truth. When she asked him if he was feeling better, he always told her yes. In reality, he was bone-tired, and could tell something was still off inside him. But she had enough to worry about without worrying about him. She was a caretaker to her soul, which made her an amazing healer, but also took a toll on her.

The last thing he ever wanted to do was take a toll on her.

"Marrick, why don't you sit down?"

He turned to her.

"And before you tell me you have to stay vigilant, we haven't seen anyone since we got here."

"That doesn't—"

"—mean there isn't someone here," she interrupted, finishing his sentence.

He couldn't hide a slight smile. "Do you have me all figured out?"

She shook her head. "Not even close."

"I'm a simple male."

It was Sam's turn to smile. "In my experience, males are very complicated."

"Is there a male in your life?" Marrick asked before he could stop himself.

Her eyes widened. "No. I...haven't had much opportunity to have serious relationships."

"Why not?" What was wrong with his tongue?

She looked down at the fire.

"Never mind. It's not my place to ask."

"It's okay. I've spent most of my life moving from place to place. I don't stay anywhere long enough to form a long-term relationship with anyone."

He cleared his voice. "You seem to be fitting in well with the Shamat clan. Maybe you can find a home there."

"Maybe."

"I'm sorry."

She looked up at him, her eyebrows pulling together as he felt her confusion.

"What are you sorry for?" Sam asked.

"For pulling you into this."

She huffed at him before standing. "*You* didn't do this. We're both stuck here, and we're going to get out of here together."

He was glad to see the longer she spent with him in his demon form, the less afraid she seemed.

And the longer he spent with Sam, the more fascinated he was. A true wonder to him.

And it was his job to protect her. To get her safely home.

Sam stared up at the infuriatingly stubborn but honorable male.

She didn't like the color of his skin. The vibrant hue had been replaced with a pale purple, and he was lying to her about feeling better. She could see it around the hard set of his eyes.

But he felt the need to protect her. Sam understood this, because she was a caretaker as well, which was in the same family as a warrior. Soldiers protected their people. But it didn't mean she wasn't irritated with him for lying.

"Let's sit down by the fire."

By the tilt of his chin, she thought he was going to fight her, but he finally sat down after she sat herself. He pushed out a hard breath.

She rested a hand on his arm. "We'll find a way home."

"I have tried to open a portal every time we've jumped to a new land, and it hasn't worked."

"That doesn't mean you won't be successful next time."

He nodded while he looked around, probably to make sure no one was sneaking up on them.

He had been so strong up to this point. If he needed a pep talk, she'd give him one. "You've forgotten your family is also fighting for you."

His gaze sharpened on her. "What do you mean?"

"Naya and the Shamat clan. They don't strike me as a group who will give up on their clan, and you're a member of their clan."

He swallowed. "I have my fellow guards, but I've never been a part of a clan before."

"Well, I think you've been adopted into one, whether you want it or not."

"The same could be said of you. The clan has opened their arms to you. You could have a family with them."

Something tightened in Sam's chest.

"I...do have a family. My mom."

He paused for a moment before responding. "Irina told me you were alone in this world."

She looked down at her hands. "It's complicated."

A large, purple hand enveloped hers. "If my parents were still alive, I would do anything to be a part of their lives."

Tears gathered in her eyes, and she blinked before looking up at him.

"I'm sorry I upset you, Sam."

She shook her head. "You didn't. I'm just worried about my mom and what she'll do..."

He squeezed her hand. "Didn't you just tell me we have a whole clan working to get us back?"

"I did. I was giving you a pep talk."

He gave her a confused look, so she explained. "It means to cheer you up."

"Ahh. Well, now it's my turn to pep you up."

Sam bumped her shoulder against his. "Sounds like a plan."

They sat together in silence, watching the fire. Sam's thoughts bounced around in her brain. Her mom would not sit quietly on the sidelines waiting for Sam to call. What if she did something?

Sam must have tensed, because Marrick squeezed her hand again. She hadn't realized he was still holding it, but when his hand enveloped hers more securely, calm settled over her. She was more than fine with that.

CHAPTER 18

Gwen didn't know what exactly was going on. She thought Boris would have locked her up, but instead she was with Irina in the community center kitchen. At first Gwen wasn't hungry, but as soon as she smelled the stewing meat and vegetables, her stomach started growling.

Irina simply smiled and handed her a loaded plate.

While they were eating, Irina filled her in on some of the events leading up to and after Sam and Marrick were sucked into the portal that Gwen didn't know about.

"Sounds like you've had a hard time convincing the Demon Council to accept the immigration."

Irina stood. "Some of them. Many are worried about allowing the clans to come to earth. I've spent time with the realm demons, and they're pretty much like us. They want a home where they have the same opportunities we do. They've been punished long enough for what their ancestors did a millennium ago."

Gwen followed Irina to the sink and silently helped her with the dishes for a few minutes until she had to ask the question that was bugging her.

"I'm surprised Boris let me be alone with you."

Irina chuckled as she wiped her hands on a kitchen towel. "Really?"

"I was expecting to be locked away after I breached the compound."

"If Boris thought you were a true threat to this clan, you wouldn't be here with me now."

"How can he be so sure?"

Irina shrugged. "We can't be sure, really. But he's not very different from you."

Gwen couldn't stop her eyebrows from popping up. "In what way?"

"He's a father who will do anything for his sons. And from what you've shown, you'll do anything for your daughter."

"I will."

Irina turned to her. "Which makes me wonder why, when I asked Sam about her family, she told me she didn't have any."

Gwen had anticipated this question, but she still struggled with an answer. Irina struck her as someone who would call bullshit if she strayed too far from the truth.

"I wanted Sam to have an opportunity to start again with this clan. I have had some issues in the past, and I didn't want to ruin this opportunity for her, so I told her not to mention me."

Irina looked at her in silence for a moment, but Gwen wasn't going to offer more at this point.

"You'll learn very quickly that this group is an eclectic mix, and we're willing to accept everyone into our clan. Sam should not feel the need to hide your existence, unless you're on a wanted poster somewhere," Irina said with a chuckle.

Gwen's stomach bottomed out, and she choked out a laugh that sounded pretty fake to her own ears.

Irina patted her arm. "Let's go find Boris."

Fine with Gwen. She wasn't sure what they were waiting for. Why weren't they doing something—anything—to bring Sam and Marrick to earth again? She followed Irina down the main hall to another hall leading to some offices. Irina tapped on a closed door and then opened it before waiting for an answer.

Boris stood from behind a desk. "By all means, Mother, come right in."

"No blustering, Son, or I won't feed you dinner."

Boris shook his head. "No time right now. Misha and Kyle are setting up the live feed in the conference room. Aleksei and Naya will be talking to Joran in a few minutes."

The Abstatholm Irina had told her about. "Why didn't you go see this Joran days ago?" Gwen asked.

Boris studied her with his startling, ice-blue eyes. "He's in a maximum-security supernatural prison. We've confirmed he's still in custody and his powers are still subdued, but we had to make special arrangements to enter the prison and interrogate him."

Irina hadn't gotten to that part of the story. "There is a prison in Cleveland?"

"No, they flew to the prison."

"Why is he in prison?"

Boris exchanged a look with Irina. "Joran was part of a group of demons who attacked this compound. He tried to kidnap my grandsons and take them to the realm."

Anger burned under Gwen's skin. "The twins Sam told me about?"

"Yes. Misha and Callie's sons."

"I'm surprised Misha doesn't want to interrogate Joran himself."

Again with the look at his mother. "He did. But I suggested he should stay here to protect his family."

"And you weren't sure if he would be able to control himself around Joran," Gwen said.

Boris's eyes narrowed. "Correct." He walked around his desk to join them. "Let's go to the conference room."

"You're going to let me listen in?" Gwen asked, not bothering to hide her surprise.

"You have a vested interest in the conversation."

"We all do," Irina chimed in.

A few doors down they entered a meeting room with a table at the front. A large male was bent over a laptop, and he looked up at them when they entered the room.

A small female sauntered over and joined them. "We're almost ready."

Boris nodded. "Kyle, this is Gwen, Sam's mother."

"Hello. The big guy behind me is Misha."

Misha stood up. His eyes were the same blue as Boris's, and he was staring at her intently.

"Have we met before?" Misha asked.

"No."

Misha watched her a moment longer before turning back to his computer. "Okay."

But his tone let her know it was far from okay.

Have we met before shouldn't be such scary words, but in Gwen's world they were terrifying. If anyone recognized her, she would be in shackles before night's end. Before that happened, she needed to make sure Sam was okay. Then they were free to do whatever they wanted to her.

———————◆○◆———————

Boris watched the petite female in front of him. There was something about her, something he knew should make him nervous. For starters, her poker face was almost too perfect.

He learned a long time ago that people who didn't show their emotions learned to do it either because they had something to hide, or because they had been hurt in the past. Which didn't sit right with him. He hoped it wasn't the case with her, but the fact that they hadn't even known she existed meant something. Maybe his mother had gotten the truth out of her. Irina could interrogate people without making them feel like it was an interrogation.

Maybe they should have sent his mother to talk to Joran.

The screen on the wall flickered and came to life with a video of Joran shackled to a table. He heard a growl from across the room, and wasn't sure if it was from his son or Kyle.

Everyone sat at the conference room table while Naya and Aleksei walked into camera view and faced Joran.

"Well, to what do I owe the pleasure?" Joran asked with a twisted grin on his face.

Aleksei stepped closer. "There have been some issues with the portal."

Joran barked out a laugh. "Issues? Is that what you call the portal shutting down?"

"How did you know?" Naya demanded.

"The immigration collapsing and burning is big news, even in prison."

Boris could see the tension pulsing from his son, even through the digital image. "You tried to stop us before and failed."

"And yet here you are, asking to see me."

"You're Abstatholm," Naya said. "You understand how the portal works."

"True."

"Have you blocked the portal?" Aleksei asked.

Joran held up his shackled arms. "How could I have done anything?"

"What about other Abstatholm on earth?" Naya asked.

"Even if I knew of someone, I sure as hell wouldn't tell you. Why would I condemn anyone else to suffer this?"

Naya crossed her arms. "You're in prison for your actions. It's too late to play the martyr."

"Insulting me isn't going to convince me to help you," Joran said.

"How can you help us if you didn't have anything to do with this?" Aleksei said.

"Me being innocent doesn't mean I can't help."

"Out of the goodness of your heart?" Aleksei said.

"I'm sure we could come to some sort of agreement. If you let me come back to the compound, I could try to help."

It was Aleksei's turn to bark out a laugh. "Not going to happen. If you didn't have anything to do with this, we're done. Guards!"

Two demons came into the room and unlocked the shackles from the table. Joran stood. "How are my dear nephews?"

Misha growled and clenched his fists on the table. Boris rested his hand on his son's shoulder.

"They aren't your family," Aleksei said.

"They're my blood. You can't deny it. That human should not be raising them. They should be with their own clan."

"They are with their own clan, and you will never get near them again."

Joran smiled. "Never is a long, long time."

"Get him out of here."

A few moments later the screen went black. They sat in silence while Boris wrestled with his urge to punch something. He wasn't sure how his son managed to simply sit at the table instead of flinging it across the room.

Kyle finally broke the silence. "Bastard."

"I think he was blowing smoke," Gwen said. "Do you think he's involved?"

"My gut tells me no," Boris said. "If something is blocking the portal from this compound like we fear, he wouldn't have been able to do it because he's been in custody. And when he was here before to kidnap Matty and Luke, he had no reason to set up some sort of fail-safe plan to shut down the portal."

Kyle leaned closer. "Agreed, but he still could have been working with someone else. So we find out if he's had any visitors."

Misha shook his head. "We already asked. He hasn't. The prison keeps records."

Gwen spoke up. "Then you need to talk to the people who are around him. Maybe there is a guard who doesn't want the immigration to continue."

"She's right. I'm going to call Naya and tell her to talk to the warden and any guards who come into direct contact with Joran." Kyle pulled out her phone and stepped to the back of the room.

Boris grasped the back of Misha's neck. Tension was still pulsing from him.

"Son, why don't you go home to Callie and the boys?"

"I should stay and help. Jean Luc and Talia are at the house with Callie and the boys. The boys have been drawing pictures to welcome Marrick and Sam back home."

Boris's heart swelled. He loved those boys. "Go home and tuck the boys into bed. We'll figure this out."

Misha shut his laptop and stood, wishing everyone a good night before studying Gwen for another long moment, as if he was trying to sort out where he'd met her. Then he left the room.

"Can I ask why Joran said he's the twins' uncle?"

"The twins' biological father was a Kelmar and Joran's brother. They came to earth to impregnate human women," Boris said.

"Why?" Gwen asked.

"Because females are not being born in the realm, and they would eventually die out there if they couldn't have children. So they came to earth."

Gwen frowned. "And the human women were okay with this?"

"In Callie's case, she didn't know he was a demon. He was killed before the twins were born, and she didn't know they were half demons until Matty created a fireball."

"Fates. That had to have been a shock."

"Yes. Luckily Misha and Kyle took them under their wing and helped her."

"And that's how she met Misha?"

"Yes. He's been a member of the Bureau of Supernatural Relations for close to a century now, and he's very good at his job. A computer expert," Boris said with a little brag in his voice.

Irina beamed. "Of course he can do all this technical stuff. His brain is a computer. He has an eidetic memory."

Was it Boris's imagination, or did Gwen's poker face slip for just a second?

Before he could think about it too much, Kyle joined them again to tell them she'd spoken to Naya, and Naya and Aleksei would be interviewing the warden and guards.

"Hopefully we'll hear from them in the morning," Boris said.

"Gwen, why don't you stay at my home tonight?" Irina said. Without waiting for an answer, she told Boris, "I'm going to go make plates for you and Kyle for dinner. When you're done talking, come to the kitchen."

"I guess I'm having dinner here and you're staying with Irina tonight," Kyle said.

Gwen looked up at Boris. "You aren't going to lock me up?"

The female intrigued Boris more and more. "Should I?"

"Maybe not. But I'm surprised you're letting me spend time with your mother."

Boris chortled at her question and Kyle laughed out loud.

"Why does everyone laugh when I ask that?"

Kyle answered. "Because Irina is one of the most powerful demons I've ever met. She can take care of herself."

Gwen nodded, and they fell silent.

"We'll get Sam back home, Gwen."

Why he needed to say that, Boris didn't know, but the tight expression on Gwen's face was a mask hiding a myriad of emotions. And he felt something close to a compulsion to reassure her.

CHAPTER 19

Marrick stood next to the tree line watching Sam while she leaned over the small stream, rinsing her face and neck off and combing her fingers through her hair. She had pulled it down from what she called a ponytail and it hung around her shoulders. He liked it loose and framing her face.

"I can feel you staring," she said without looking up.

"I'm just keeping watch."

She turned and grinned at him. "Shouldn't you be looking out there instead of at me?"

Her adorable expression punched him in the gut. "You never know what might be lurking in the stream."

She laughed and stood up, pulling her hair back together and tying it with the stretchy band she had around her wrist.

"By all means, we should move away from the scary water, then." But when she glanced over his shoulder, her smile changed to a frown.

Before he could turn, he felt the familiar pull and knew a portal had opened behind him. "Sam!"

Sam ran up the bank and reached for him. Her wet fingers slipped through his grip, and he lurched forward even as the portal tried to swallow him. He grabbed her wrist.

"Don't let me go."

He tightened his grip. "Never."

They flew backward into the abyss, and the air was sucked out of his lungs, but he held onto Sam while they twisted and were finally spit out into a new world, this time landing on the ground.

Marrick sat up and turned to Sam, who lay next to him. "Are you okay?"

"Yeah." She blew out a shaky breath. "But I don't think I'll ever get used to that."

Marrick struggled to his feet and reached for her, pulling her to stand next to him. He turned and looked around—and his heart started to pound.

"What is it?" Sam asked.

He turned back to her and grabbed her shoulders.

"What's wrong?"

"We're in the realm!"

"You're sure?"

"Yes. I recognize the forest across the meadow and"—he drew in a deep breath—"the air."

She gaped up at him in disbelief. He could barely believe it himself.

"Try to contact Naya. Maybe she'll hear you now that we're in the realm."

He closed his eyes and concentrated for a moment to get his thoughts to stop bouncing all over the place.

Naya, can you hear me?

He waited for a moment, his stomach sinking at the silence.

Naya?

Marrick! Thank the fates. Where are you?

He grinned down at Sam and nodded. And then he chuckled at the little dance she did around him.

We're in the realm. We just landed here.

Is Sam with you? Are you both okay?

Yes, she's with me. We're both fine. We haven't been able to control the portal, which has sent us to several different lands.

We've been trying to find you. Aleksei and I interrogated Joran to see if he was involved.

He felt a tap on his arm and opened his eyes.

"What is she saying?"

"She asked me where we've been, and then told me they went to talk to Joran to see if he had anything to do with sending us through the portal."

"Did he?"

"I don't know. You interrupted me."

She pursed her lips, and he stifled the urge to laugh. He knew she wouldn't appreciate it.

Marrick?

Sorry. Sam's asking me what's going on, so I'm going to need to tell her what we're talking about as we go along. Did you get anything from Joran?

Not much. He said he had nothing to do with it. Just to be safe, we're interrogating the guards at the prison. Something is off, but we haven't figured out what yet.

He looked down at Sam. "Naya says they didn't get much from him. They're trying to figure out if someone is working with him."

We're going to see if we can get more information about how Abstatholms' powers work. We spoke to Lela, but she couldn't tell us much about them since they are somewhat secretive. Since you're in the realm, maybe you can visit the Kelmar village and get more information as well. Lela suggested speaking with her father, Saboll.

We can do that, and we're close to the village. We'll head there shortly.

He relayed the information to Sam, who nodded.

Naya's voice filled his head. *Oh, I almost forgot. Sam's mother is here. She hadn't heard from Sam, so she came to find out what's wrong. She actually kind of stormed the compound and gave Boris a talking-to about finding her daughter.*

He looked over at Sam, who was watching him with a curious look on her face. *Okay, I'll contact you once we're at the Kelmar village.*

I'll reach out to Krell to see if any of the guards can meet you there. Have you tried to initiate the portal?

I tried every time we landed somewhere new and it never worked. I don't want to try now since I'm afraid it might take us to another place. We're safe here.

Agreed. It's so good to hear from you, my friend. Stay in touch.

He said his goodbyes to Naya and turned to Sam.

"What were you talking about at the end?" Sam asked.

"Your mother is at the Shamat compound."

The color drained from her face as fear surged from her with an intensity that almost knocked him back a step.

"What's wrong?"

Sam shook her head back and forth. "She can't be at the compound."

"Naya said she was worried when she couldn't get ahold of you. So she came to find you."

"Tell Naya I'm fine and my mom can leave."

"Sam—"

"Tell her!"

Marrick held up his hands. "There is obviously something wrong that you don't feel you can tell me about."

"No."

"Please help me understand."

"She shouldn't be at the Shamat compound. It's not safe for her," Sam blurted, and then cringed at her words.

"Why, Sam?"

She looked away from him as confusion and fear pulsed from her. He wasn't sure if she was going to tell him the truth.

She finally blew out a breath. "My mother is wanted for a crime she didn't commit. If they figure out who she is, they'll arrest her. She needs to leave now."

He hadn't known what to expect, but certainly it wasn't that.

"That's why you told everyone you don't have a family."

"Yes. You need to tell her to leave."

He stared into her troubled face. "Are you sure? Think about what you're saying. Don't you think they'll question why you're telling her to leave? As it is, they're probably already suspicious about why you told us you don't have any family."

Sam blinked and his stomach twisted at the tear trickling down her cheek. "I don't care what they think of me. I want her safe."

"Okay. I can tell Naya you want your mother to leave. But let me ask you, do you think she will?"

Another tear tracked down her cheek. "No. She won't leave. Not until I'm back on earth. She'll risk herself for me."

"Because she loves you."

"Yes." Sam started pacing in front of him. "And because she is the most stubborn demon on the planet. Well...the planet earth. You know what I mean."

"I do. Why don't we visit the Kelmar village and see if they have any ideas about how the portal could be blocked? If we can find a way to get home, your mother can be on her way before anyone recognizes her."

Sam nodded. He headed in the direction of the village as she fell in step beside him.

"This is where you live?"

"My home is in the in-between. It's a place where the guards live when we aren't on duty."

"And you've spent your whole life here. Did you ever think about coming back to earth?"

"My family was here, and my duty. I didn't know anything else."

"Until recently."

"Yes, seeing what earth has to offer has opened my eyes to new possibilities for my future. Once the last demon who wants to leave here has come to earth, I will see about settling there myself."

She stopped and faced him. "But it could take years."

"Yes, but I want to see it through."

She blinked up at him. "You're a good male, Marrick."

They lapsed into silence and continued walking while he let her sort out her thoughts. She had been through so much because of him, and he wanted to find a way to get her home safely.

They arrived in the Kelmar village a couple of hours later, and the Kelmar came out of their huts to greet them. Saboll, the Kelmar ruler, held out his arm to Marrick, who grasped his forearm in greeting.

"We were told by the guard that you were trapped on earth. Does this mean the portal has been fixed?"

"Not exactly. Which is why we're here to ask for your help." Marrick beckoned for Sam join them. "This is Sam."

Saboll bowed slightly. "Welcome. May I ask if Lela is well?"

"Yes, she's fine. In fact, she's the one who suggested we come discuss it with you."

Saboll beckoned for them to follow him. "Let's get you both some food and water, and we'll see what we can do to help."

They settled in front of a fire and ate a wonderful meal. Sam actually groaned in appreciation, and a moment later her face turned red.

Saboll gave her a friendly nod. "That is a great compliment. I will make sure to tell Denal his food was well received." He set his own plate down. "Now we've had our meal, let's talk about how our clan can help."

Marrick filled him in on what had happened so far before he began asking questions. "We've been wondering if you can explain what Abstatholm are capable of?"

Saboll leaned back and seemed to consider his words. "The Abstatholm are not very forthcoming about their powers. I understand to a certain extent, since they have not wanted to be taken advantage of. It's a shame some of them used their powers to take advantage of others. I do know they can travel great distances, both in the realm and beyond."

"Have they been to other worlds besides earth?"

"I believe so, yes. Although no one has confirmed this for me. I don't think they're restricted to just following the portal to earth. Over the centuries we've been aware of Abstatholm leaving the realm, and many assumed they went to earth, but I'm not convinced."

"Do you think they can block the portal?" Sam asked.

"Their power is based on the ebb and flow of energy. It makes sense that they could interrupt the portal as well. I just don't know. I think you need to discuss this with Tarat. He's an Abstatholm who lives a couple of hours from here. He prefers to live on his own."

Marrick leaned forward. "He's willing to talk to us?"

"Yes, I'll have to talk to him first. I'll send one of the clan to bring him back here."

Marrick almost argued that he should be the one to go to Tarat, but Sam looked like she was ready to fall asleep, and he wasn't doing much better.

"Why don't you both stay for the night? Tarat should arrive here late tomorrow morning."

"We're grateful for your offer of accommodations for the night."

With a gracious smile Saboll led them to a hut across from the fire. "This should work for the night. There are blankets and a cot. I'll see about bringing you both some fresh clothes."

"We don't want to impose," Sam said.

"You're not imposing. Now we have clothes from earth, we have plenty of supplies. I'll see what we can find for both of you."

Saboll left them outside the hut, and they went inside. There was a cot on one side of the room, and the other held a table and a fireplace with kindling. He went over and squatted down to start the fire.

"An actual cot," Sam said as she took in the small space. "I would lie down on it right now if I wasn't so dirty."

"I'll heat up some water so you can wash, but it will take a bit of time."

Sam's face lit up, and it warmed his heart.

"How are you feeling?" Sam asked.

"I'm tired, but I think it's more from not sleeping."

She crossed her arms. "I told you I can keep watch just as well as you can."

"I know."

Her lips pursed again in that cute way she had. "Are you placating me right now?"

"Of course not," but he couldn't stifle his amusement.

Sam's eyes danced. "You're in trouble, buster."

A knock at the door stopped him from responding to her. "Come in."

Saboll walked in carrying some clothes, closely followed by two demons carrying pots of hot water.

"We thought you might like to bathe."

"Thank you *so* much," Sam said.

They were soon left alone. "I'll step outside."

"Why don't you take the second pot of water with you while it's hot?"

She held up her hand before he could argue, went to the clothes, and pulled out a shirt and pants for him, telling him to hold out his arms so she could stack the clothes there. She then broke the small bar of soap in half and set it on top of his clothes.

"All set."

"You are stubborn, female."

"Thank you. I'll take that as a compliment. Now, shoo."

He looked down at his feet.

She laughed. "It's not *that* kind of shoe. It means 'go away.'"

Marrick shifted the clothes to one arm and lifted the pot of water before heading out the door, where Saboll invited him to use his own hut to clean up and change clothes. Afterward, he settled down outside by the communal fire.

A few minutes later Sam peeked her head out of the hut and waved at him. He went over to her.

"I was wondering where you were."

"I was going to sleep outside by the fire tonight."

"Don't be silly. We've been sleeping next to each other for more than a week. You'll be more comfortable in here." She opened the door wider. "See? I made a bed for one of us on the floor."

"I'll take the floor," Marrick said. After the look on her face earlier when she saw the cot, there was no way he would let her sleep on the ground.

She settled on the cot, and he stoked the fire before lying down on the floor next to her. The firelight cast shadows along the walls, and they lay in silence, the sounds of their breathing filling the small hut.

"Will you tell me about your power?" Sam asked quietly, as if the darkness called for soft voices.

He couldn't see her face, although he could read her, and he sensed more curiosity than revulsion. "I developed my ability as a child. It confused me at first. I didn't understand why the adults around me would act one way when they were feeling the opposite."

"It has to be hard to know what others are feeling."

He wasn't surprised she understood his struggles. "Yes. I feel like I'm invading others' privacy."

"And it's hard enough to deal with our own feelings on top of someone else's."

He looked over at the fire for a moment before responding. "I've learned to block much of it out."

"That has to be hard too. Always on guard."

He sat up and could barely make out her profile in the firelight. "Thank you for understanding."

"I used to be jealous of demons who had powers. I didn't realize they aren't all a blessing."

"Sam, you do have a power," Marrick said.

She turned toward him. "What do you mean?"

"I think you're empathic too, but in a different way. You are a great nurse, and part of what you do is share your feelings with others. Calm, security, confidence. It helps the people you are taking care of face their fears."

"As a nurse, you learn how to stay calm in a crisis."

"It's more than that. When you rested your hand on my chest in the hospital, a sense of calm flowed from you to me. And I saw how Luke calmed down immediately when you touched him after his fall."

"I don't know," Sam said.

Marrick wanted to reach out and wrap his arm around her. Instead, he did the next best thing. "I know this has been hard, but I promise to get you home."

Firelight illuminated her beautiful face and his heart expanded.

"I'm happy we got you home," Sam said. "Now we're in the realm, I'm sure we'll figure out how to get the portal working again."

He was feeling more confident as well. As long as the portal didn't open and pull him inside.

If it did, he would not take Sam with him this time. He had no idea where the next jump would take him, and he knew she would be safe here. Naya and the Shamat clan wouldn't rest until they were able to save Sam and start the immigration again.

He was not important.

CHAPTER 20

Gwen woke the next morning to the smell of something decadent. Sam hadn't exaggerated about what a fantastic cook Irina was.

She looked at the twin bed Sam had been sleeping in. Her pajamas were folded at the foot, and Gwen couldn't bring herself to move any of her daughter's belongings. She would be back here soon enough if Gwen had anything to say about it.

Irina had loaned her a nightgown for the night, which she quickly changed out of and into her clothes from yesterday. She would have to see if Boris would be okay with her going to the rental car she'd hidden in the woods to grab her duffel bag. Even though she'd stayed with Irina last night, it didn't mean she was free to move about the compound—or leave it, for that matter.

She spent a few minutes freshening up in the bathroom before she headed to the kitchen.

"Hello, dear. You're just in time. The cinnamon rolls are warm."

"They smell amazing."

Irina waved her hand for Gwen to take a seat. "I promised the twins I would make them. They've been so upset about Marrick and Sam disappearing, I decided to do something to cheer them up."

"You have a tight-knit family."

"We do. Boris and his sons mean the world to me. And now all three boys have found their mates, and they have become my granddaughters. And of course, now I have great-grandchildren too!"

Gwen couldn't imagine what it must feel like to be part of a large family. "You're very lucky."

"I thank the Fates every day."

"Misha adores the twins."

"He does, Callie likes to say he fell in love with them before her. My grandsons love with all their hearts. They learned it from their father."

As if Irina's words summoned him, Boris burst through the back kitchen door.

Irina grabbed her chest. "Boris! What in the world!"

"Sorry. I had to come tell you. Marrick and Sam are in the realm!"

Gwen jumped up, having trouble taking a complete breath.

Irina clapped her hands together. "Thank goodness!"

"How do you know?" Gwen choked out.

"Naya is telepathic. When Marrick and Sam arrived in the realm, he was able to reach her."

"Sam's okay?"

"Yes, they both are. We were right. They were pulled to different worlds until they finally made their way to the realm."

"How do we get them back to earth?" Gwen asked.

"We'll figure it out. Sam and Marrick have gone to the Kelmar village to ask about the Abstatholm and whether they have the ability to block the portal, and Naya and Aleksei are on their way back from interviewing the guards at the prison.

"We're calling a meeting in a couple hours to talk through next steps, and I'm sure we'll come up with a plan."

Gwen blew out the breath she'd been holding. "Okay."

Irina set a roll in front of Boris and then reached for her phone and excused herself for a moment, leaving them alone.

Gwen needed to pull herself together. First priority was getting her daughter home before someone figured out who she was.

"Are you okay?" Boris asked.

She schooled her expression before looking at him again. "Yes. Thanks for coming to tell us."

"Absolutely. As soon as Naya called, I wanted to let you know."

Gwen just looked at him. She wasn't sure what she'd done to earn his compassion. She'd broken into his compound, for one thing, and basically told him off for another. Not the best first impression.

Before she could say anything, Irina came back into the kitchen.

"Callie and the boys are on their way over. All I had to say was 'warm cinnamon rolls' and the boys were running toward the door." Irina chuckled.

Gwen grinned. "Sam told me about them. They sound adorable."

"They are. But you'll experience it for yourself in a minute or less."

A knock at her front door was followed by thundering footsteps.

"BB!" voices called out before they careened into the kitchen. Two boys stopped and looked at her. They were green-eyed, and both had sandy mops of hair.

"Gwen, these are my great-grandsons, Matty and Luke. Say hi, boys."

"Hi," they both said.

"You're Sam's momma," the twin on the right said.

"Yes."

They both went to her and patted her hand. "We like Sam and Marrick," the twin to the left said.

"We all do, Matty," Irina said.

Gwen swallowed the lump in her throat. They were being so sweet. And now she knew who was who, she could see Luke was holding what looked like some sort of art project.

"What's that?"

"It's a book," Luke said. "Momma helped us put our drawings together. It's for Sam and Marrick."

"Do you want to see it?" Matty asked.

"Yes."

Gwen paged carefully through the crayon drawings. Each had a purple male and a female with a ponytail standing in the middle of different outdoor scenes. "This is really good."

The boys grinned.

"We wanted to make them a welcome home gift."

"Well, this is a wonderful gift. Sam will love it."

"Boys!" a voice called out from the front of the house.

"Did you run away from your momma?" Irina asked.

They both looked down before mumbling, "Maybe."

"But you said the cinnamon rolls were *warm*!" Luke exclaimed.

Gwen bit her lips to keep from laughing, and she could tell from Boris's eyes that he was also trying not to laugh.

A petite blond stomped into the kitchen looking frustrated.

"Sorry, Momma!" they chorused.

She rested her hands on their heads. "Next time you wait for me."

"Yes, ma'am."

"Don't bat those green eyes at me, boys. I'm serious."

"Miss Gwen says our book is really good," Matty said.

Gwen was impressed to note they were already skilled at changing the subject.

Callie looked up and smiled at Gwen. "Hi, I'm Callie."

"Nice to meet you."

Irina wrangled the boys and Callie into seats at the table and put rolls in front of the boys along with glasses of milk, and they dug into them.

Boris kept trying to steal the rolls from the boys' plates, which triggered giggles.

"Grandpa!"

"Do you want some tea, Callie?" Irina asked.

"Please." She turned to Gwen. "We heard the good news that Marrick and Sam are in the realm now."

"Yes, thank the Fates," Gwen said.

Irina set the teacup in front of Callie. "Now we just need to get them back to earth and fix the portal so the immigration can continue."

"We'll figure it out," Callie said.

"You're very confident," Gwen said.

"I've seen what this clan can do," Callie said with conviction.

"Papa will get them home," Luke said.

"And Aunt Kyle," Matty said.

"And Aunt Naya and Uncle Aleksei," Luke continued.

"And?" Boris asked.

"And Grandpa!" the boys shouted.

Boris kissed Matty on the head and then Luke. "Good answer."

Gwen was stunned to see the love this male felt for the two little boys who weren't his blood. This family took in total strangers, as they had with Sam. Gwen knew she'd made the right decision sending Sam here. No matter what happened to her, Sam had found a new family who would take care of her.

CHAPTER 21

Sam woke up when she heard shouts outside the hut. Marrick was on his feet before she could even get her bearings.

"Wait here until I find out what's going on."

He opened the hut door just as someone ran past them. "What happened?"

"There's been an accident."

Sam pulled on her shoes and tied her hair back as she rushed to the door. "Come on, they probably need help."

They emerged from the hut to see several demons carrying a male into a hut at the end of the row. Sam jogged toward the building with Marrick right beside her.

Saboll nodded to them as he stood outside the hut.

"Who's hurt?" Sam asked.

"Palan was planting and cut his leg on the plow blade."

"I'm a nurse. Let me help. Do you have a healer?"

"Thoman is inside."

Sam entered the hut and saw a male holding gauze over the injured demon's leg.

"I'm Sam. I'm a nurse and can help. I understand you're the healer."

"I've been training with Sabrina when she visits, but this..."

"It's okay. We'll work together."

Sam could tell from the amount of blood coming through the gauze the cut was bad and had more than likely hit an artery. She yelled for Marrick and Saboll, who burst into the hut together. "Saboll, I need you to find me something to stop the bleeding. A tourniquet. A belt and something long and thin like a branch."

Saboll nodded before running back outside.

"Marrick, come here and take over applying pressure on his leg."

Marrick knelt and pushed down on the gauze, making Palan groan.

Sam laid her hand on Palan's shoulder, trying to reassure him. If what Marrick had said was true, her touch might calm Palan, and she'd do anything to help calm him. She spent a second attempting to push calming thoughts to him. "Sorry, I know it hurts. Thoman, can you show me where the supplies are?"

He pointed to the cabinet along the wall. As soon as she opened the cabinet door, Sam was relieved to see Sabrina had stocked it with medical-grade supplies. She pulled out a suture kit and some instruments, and set them on the table next to the cot.

Saboll ran back into the room with a thin leather belt and a sturdy branch.

"That should work. Thanks."

She looked at Thoman, Marrick, and then Palan. "I'm going to tell you all what I'm doing while I work, okay? We're going to get through this together. Are you ready?"

When they all nodded, she bent over her patient and got to work.

An hour later, she sat back after taking Palan's vitals. He was doing well now they had sutured the artery and leg shut. His demon metabolism should kick in now that he wasn't losing so much blood, and would heal him in the next couple of days.

Palan had fallen asleep, which would help with the healing as well. She looked up at Thoman and smiled. "You did a great job," she said softly.

"You saved him."

"We all saved him." She looked over her shoulder just as Marrick and Saboll entered the hut. Marrick had remained through the whole ordeal, until she had sent him outside to tell Saboll that Palan was going to be fine. She stood and wobbled a little bit. Marrick was by her side in a second.

"I'm okay. My legs cramped up from being down on the ground so long."

"You need a break."

Before she could protest, Saboll spoke up. "I'll watch Palan. Why don't you all go get cleaned up and have something to eat and drink?"

Sam nodded as they went outside, Thoman heading in one direction with Marrick and Sam going back to the hut they'd stayed in the night before.

"Saboll said they put fresh clothes here for us, as well as some water to clean up."

Which was a good thing, since her hands and arms were still covered with Palan's blood.

"You were amazing, Sam."

She felt her face heat at his praise. "I was just doing my job."

"Which doesn't make you any less amazing."

She grabbed a rag and dipped it in the bucket, cleaning her arms and hands with the warm water. "Thankfully Sabrina had stocked the village with top-notch medical supplies, or we would have been in trouble."

"Not only has Sabrina been setting up healing facilities in the villages, she's been training healers as well."

"I'll have to talk to her about adding some trauma classes to her trainings."

He smiled, and she almost dropped the rag at the intensity of it. "What?"

"You're trapped in the realm and your first thought is how you can help the demons here."

Her face heated again. She was pretty sure she was bright red now.

"Amazing."

"Stop saying that." Time to change the subject. "Give me a moment to wash and change and then you can come back in and do the same."

He nodded and went outside.

Fifteen minutes later they were both cleaned up, and Sam peeked in on Palan to make sure he was still okay before they sat down at the main fire.

Across from them a tall, thin demon watched them carefully. After a moment, he stood and brought them a water jug and two clay mugs.

"Thank you," Sam said.

"We should be thanking you. I understand you helped save Palan's life."

"It was a group effort."

"May I sit next to you?"

"Sure."

He sat down and gazed into the fire for a few moments. Sam looked over at Marrick in question. He shrugged slightly.

Finally the demon spoke. "I understand you want to ask me some questions."

"Tarat?" Marrick guessed.

"Yes."

"Thank you for coming to talk to us," Sam said.

"Honestly, I wasn't planning to do it. Out of respect for Saboll, I agreed to come to the village, but I didn't promise him I would talk to you."

"What changed your mind?"

"Seeing you save Palan even when you don't know for sure if the Kelmar are responsible for blocking the portal."

Sam shook her head. "I would never blame a clan for the actions of one or two individuals." But hadn't she been doing that very thing with the Pavel?

Tarat looked down at his hands. "We Abstatholm do not discuss our powers freely. Knowledge is power, and it can be used against us."

Marrick leaned forward. "Understandable. But if an Abstatholm is blocking the portal, the immigration cannot continue, and everyone is trapped. We need to figure out how to make the portal work again."

Tarat gazed into the fire for a moment while Sam held her breath. He could easily walk away and not tell them anything.

"Explain to me what happened," Tarat said.

Marrick described what happened when the portal shut down. He then told Tarat about getting sucked into the portal. Tarat perked up when Marrick talked about the various worlds they had visited.

"And you had no control over the portal?"

"None. It would open up unexpectedly and yank us to another world."

"What were they like?"

Both Sam and Marrick talked about the various lands. Tarat listened quietly until they finished.

"Can the Abstatholm go to other places besides earth and the realm?" Sam asked.

Tarat smiled slightly and looked around to make sure there were no other clansmen nearby. "Energy flows along different pathways, and the paths can lead to other destinations."

"And you can open the portal at will?" Marrick asked.

"Yes."

"What about blocking the energies?" Marrick continued.

Tarat frowned. "It is much easier to move with energy than to push against it."

"But it can be done?" Sam asked.

"Somewhat."

"How?"

"Energy can either attract or repel other energy."

"Like energy repels and opposite energy attracts, kind of like a magnet," Sam said.

Marrick's eyes widened at her response.

Sam smiled at his reaction. "What? I've studied science and biology for years."

Tarat nodded. "She is correct."

"And you think that's what happened when I went into the portal?"

"From what you described, it spit you right back out again. I don't know if the portal was blocked as much as it repelled you instead."

"How?" Sam asked.

"There are conduits that increase energy and could have been enough to affect the portal."

"Like the red crystals?" she asked.

"What an interesting question."

"We thought the red crystals might play a part in your powers."

Marrick pulled the crystal hanging around his neck from under his shirt. "Could this play a part in it?"

"May I see it?" Tarat asked.

Marrick pulled the crystal necklace off and handed it to Tarat, who ran his fingers over the crystal itself. "I don't feel anything out of the ordinary. Do you always wear it?"

"Yes, and I've never had problems before."

"Someone had to have started this reaction."

"We only know of one Abstatholm on earth right now, and his powers have been dampened," Marrick said.

"Joran was wrong in what he did," Tarat said. "If his powers have been muted, then I don't think he would have the ability to do this."

"So someone else had to have blocked it."

Tarat nodded. "I would venture to suggest that there are more than one Abstatholm on earth right now. But they aren't going to admit it outright. May I touch your arm to find out if I can sense anything else?"

Tarat held out his hand, and Marrick grabbed it.

After a few moments, Tarat's eyes widened. "You have traces of Abstatholm energy running through you."

"How is that possible?" Sam asked.

"I don't know. I've never seen this before. Have you been near Joran recently?"

"No."

"Then you were exposed to another Abstatholm, who infected your body with energy. It could be clashing with your portal device, which might have started the issues."

"Can you form a portal to send us back to earth?" Sam asked.

"When we heard the portal was blocked, Saboll came to me and asked me to attempt to create a portal. I wasn't able to summon enough energy to create the gateway."

"But if what you say happened to me, why is it blocking everyone else's ability to open the portal?"

Tarat thought for a moment before responding. "Think of energy as being connected." He intertwined his fingers. "If one strand has been impacted, it will impact those around it. So those who travel between the realm and earth are also impacted."

"And traveling to other worlds?"

"Those portal journeys to other worlds are fascinating."

"The energy had to go somewhere," Sam said. They both looked at her, and she continued. "Energy is always there. If the energy can't complete its path or trajectory, it will need to take another path, since it can't die."

Tarat smiled at her. "Precisely. The energy was building in Marrick, and when it finally reached its limit, it had to expend itself."

"So how do we fix it?" Marrick said.

Tarat rubbed his hands on his pants legs. "You need to determine who the Abstatholm is who started this, and have them open the portal and bring you back to earth."

CHAPTER 22

Boris looked around the conference room table at his family. As the leader of the immigration, Aleksei sat at the head, and Boris to his right. Misha sat next to him, and Irina and Gwen across from them.

Naya stood with Kara in her arms, rocking her back and forth while his granddaughter giggled. From the way she was holding onto Naya, she'd missed her momma and daddy while they were at the prison. Then Sabrina joined them and sat down as well.

"Where's the rest of the BSR team?" Boris asked.

"Kyle, Jean Luc, and Jason are on their way here. We can get them up to speed later," Misha said.

"Did you find out anything more at the prison, Aleksei?" Irina asked.

"Not much. We interviewed the warden and the guards, but we couldn't find enough of a connection between Joran and any of them to suspect they helped cause this."

"So we're back to square one?" Boris asked, looking around at the people in the room, all wearing the same grim expression he probably had as well...except Naya. She had a far-off look on her face.

"Naya, are you talking to Marrick?" Aleksei asked.

"Yes."

Boris stood and took Kara in his arms so Naya could concentrate on what Marrick was telling her.

And then they sat in silence...with the exception of Kara, who grabbed onto Boris's face and patted it, squealing at him.

"I love you too, beautiful girl." He felt eyes on him, and he looked across the table at Gwen, who watched him closely, her tight expression giving nothing away.

After a few more minutes, Naya blinked and refocused on the table. "Marrick and Sam are in the Kelmar village, and they spoke to an Abstatholm. Let me fill you in on what they learned."

She spoke for several minutes, explaining things with no one interrupting her until she started talking about the other lands Marrick and Sam had visited.

"Wait," Gwen said. "Did you say blue trees?"

"And orange rivers, why?"

Gwen gaped. "Because I've seen those."

"Where?" Boris asked.

She looked over at Misha. "In the book the twins made for Marrick and Sam. They drew blue trees in one picture and an orange river in another."

Misha pushed back his chair and stood. "You think the twins had something to do with this?"

She looked up at him. "I don't believe in coincidence."

Boris stood and put his hand on Misha's shoulder. "Gwen's not blaming the boys. But what if what Naya told us is true? Something caused the portal to malfunction, and Marrick somehow has Abstatholm energy running through him. He only travels to this compound from the realm. Who could have gotten close to him outside of this clan? We've known the boys might be Abstatholm for a while now."

"If they were adults, maybe. They're seven years old!"

"Exactly," Naya said. "Which means if they *are* developing the powers to create a portal, they wouldn't understand it."

"But why now?" Misha said.

"For many demons, their powers are triggered by something," Sabrina said. "The twins have been spending quite a bit of time with Marrick. Maybe he has residual energies from his portal transfers that somehow jump-started their own powers."

Misha's face went pale. "Marrick opened a portal at my house. The boys were in the other room, but of course they could have felt the energy."

Sabrina nodded. "That could have done it. They also spent time with him prior to when he opened the portal when he was injured."

"Yes," Boris said. "They were practically sitting in his lap, explaining all the foods to him at dinner that night."

"Wouldn't Lela feel something if their energy changed?" Naya asked.

"Lela hasn't been around the twins. She hasn't been feeling well," Sabrina said.

"Sabrina, what's wrong with Lela?" Boris said, his heart speeding up.

"She's fine. Worn down. I told her to take it easy for a while, and Sergei is watching over her."

"Now what?" Aleksei said.

Sabrina stood. "I used my healing senses on Luke the other day when he fell, but I didn't feel anything different. I can try again to see if I feel anything."

"Let's do that, but we have someone else who might be able to help." Misha picked up his phone and hit a button. "Kyle, I need you to pick up Galim and bring him to the compound as soon as possible. I'll explain everything once you get here."

Forty minutes later the group stood around the table looking down at the crayon drawings the twins had made. Misha had gone to the house and explained what was going on to Callie, and brought the book back with him. Naya communicated with Marrick and confirmed that the drawings were representations of the different worlds they had visited.

The BSR team had arrived with Galim as well, and was now brought up to speed.

Callie walked in with the boys, who looked around at the crowd of people in the room before looking at the pages on the table.

"Our book!" Matty said.

"Why did you pull it apart?" Luke said.

Misha hunkered down in front of them. "It's okay, boys, it can be fixed again. Can you tell us how you came up with these drawings?"

They looked at each other before answering. "Dreams."

"You dreamed about all these places?" Misha asked.

"Yes. Is that bad?" Luke said.

Callie wrapped her arms around her sons' shoulders. "No, babies. We're just trying to figure some things out about Sam and Marrick."

"Are they coming home?" Matty asked.

"We're working on it right now, and we need your help," Misha said.

"We'll help, Papa," they both said, and Boris's eyes burned at the sincerity shining on their faces.

Boris looked at Galim.

"I can feel the energy," Galim confirmed.

"Come here, boys. We have some things to talk about," Misha said, before holding out his arms and enveloping them in his embrace.

Irina wrapped her arm around Callie, who was watching with tears in her eyes.

Boris locked his legs to stop from grabbing his son and grandsons in a hug himself. What in the Fates were they going to do now?

———————◆○◆▬▬———————

Marrick couldn't have heard Naya correctly. Something must be wrong with her telepathy.

Can you repeat that?

We think the twins are the ones who accidentally damaged the portal. Galim confirmed that their Abstatholm powers have emerged.

How are they going to open the portal to bring us home?

We're working on it now. I'll let you know what we're doing as soon as I can.

Don't let those boys get hurt, Naya. Bringing us to earth isn't worth the boys' safety.

Agreed. We'll talk soon.

Marrick squatted and stoked the fire in the hut they were using. Sam was in the healer's hut checking on Palan, which gave him a few minutes to think through what Naya just told him. The twins were Abstatholm. Those boys were already more powerful than most demons, and they were only seven.

Marrick stood as Sam entered the hut.

"Palan is doing well." The smile she wore dropped off her face when she looked at him. "What's wrong?"

Marrick repeated what Naya told him, and Sam sank onto the cot as she listened.

"I didn't think this experience could get any stranger, but here we are." She frowned. "Bringing us back might not be safe for the boys. Tell Naya not to risk them if they can't do it safely."

Could this female be any more kindhearted? "I already told her something similar."

"Do you think we should talk to Tarat? Maybe he has some advice."

"We'll talk to him in the morning. He agreed to stay in the village for a few more days in case we needed to talk to him, and I saw him turn in an hour or so ago. With the way time moves faster here, it could be a couple days before we hear from Naya again."

She nodded before she took her shoes off and pulled her hair out of the ponytail so her brown hair cascaded around her shoulders. She fascinated him more than any female he'd ever met. Which excited and scared him at the same time.

"I like your hair down," he said before he could stop himself.

"Uh...thanks," she said, her face and neck turning pink. "It gets in the way when I'm working."

"Well, you're not working now."

"No." She looked at him. "The same can't be said of you, right? You're always working, aren't you?"

"When I'm in the realm, yes. Sometimes when I'm in my hut in the in-between, I can relax."

She chuckled. "I don't see you as the lounging type."

"What type do you see me as?" Fates, why had he asked such a question?

"Serious."

Which didn't sound very encouraging.

She continued. "Kindhearted, honest, loyal."

Good traits, but all were traits of a friend or brother.

"Protective."

At this point he almost groaned at her words.

"Funny."

He perked up.

"Stubborn, exasperating, caring—and cute." Her pink face turned red as she rushed to say the last words.

"I'm not sure my human face is *that* cute," he said. He'd stayed in his demon form since they were sucked into the portal so he could protect her.

"Your demon form is pretty nice, too."

His eyebrows popped up as if they had a mind of their own. Over the course of the time they'd been together, she had become more comfortable with his demon side and no longer flinched if he came near.

Now *his* face heated, and he imagined his purple cheeks were turning magenta.

She laughed. "You aren't used to compliments, are you?"

"Neither are you. If someone tells you you're a good nurse, you say you're just doing your job."

"I am."

"Yes, but you bring some special qualities to it. You're compassionate and bighearted, which makes you a good nurse. You're also smart and confident and stand up for yourself."

She looked away from him.

"You're trying really hard right now not to deny it, aren't you?"

She tilted her head. "Yes. I don't know why I feel the need to do it."

"Well, you're also stubborn, exasperating, and caring," he said, repeating her own words back to her.

"And?" she asked.

He couldn't get the word *cute* to form on his lips. "And beautiful. It steals my breath when I gaze at you for too long."

Her jaw dropped, and there was the delectable pink face again. He took a step closer and turned into his human form. He wanted to touch her, and even though she was more at ease with his demon form, he didn't want to risk scaring her off.

He lifted his hand slowly and rested his palm against her cheek. Her skin was soft, and he caressed her, running his fingers lightly along her jawline.

She closed her eyes and leaned into his touch—and again he had trouble breathing. "Sam." She opened her eyes and gazed at him with a warmth he'd never experienced.

"I want to kiss you. Can I?"

He could see her pulse flutter in her neck before she nodded. He leaned closer, slowly, giving her time to change her mind, even though his body screamed for him to hurry up. His lips finally, finally brushed against hers.

It was like the first time he saw the mountain vista to the south, or the massive trees in the western forest towering above him, making him feel a part of something magnificent. But this was even better. It was what he thought perfection should be, and he could easily become addicted.

He wanted to wrap his arms around her and pull her in tight. Instead he kissed her lightly one more time and stepped back.

Sam blinked and took a deep breath, which made him want to stick out his chest and yell with masculine pride.

He smiled at her. "Was that okay?"

"Absolutely. You?"

He tucked her hair behind her ear. "It was amazing. And as much I would like to continue, I think we should get some sleep so we can talk to Tarat in the morning."

Sam sat down on the cot. "Do you think this will all be over soon?"

"We're closer than ever before, Sam. I promised to find a way to get you home, and I will."

And he meant it, more than any promise he'd ever made before. More and more he realized *she* was what mattered. Being a guard for him had always meant a willingness to sacrifice for his fellow guards. In the past he would have died for Naya or any of his guard family.

Now? Now, he had an aching need to protect this female who invaded his thoughts day and night. Not only would he sacrifice his life for her, but his soul as well.

CHAPTER 23

Boris looked around the room while they talked about options. After Misha explained things to the boys, they understood way more than Boris expected them to.

Callie had taken the boys home to rest while the group tossed around ideas, including having Sergei absorb their powers and open the portal himself, since he could do it by using other demons' powers. The problem with that option was the twins had never opened a portal, so the actual ability could not be transferred to him.

Naya had explained the suggestions from Tarat in the realm, but they were still leery about letting the twins try it on their own. And Marrick had told Naya that neither he nor Sam wanted to endanger the boys, so they shouldn't open the portal.

Boris had watched Gwen's face while Naya had announced that little tidbit. Her eyes flared slightly, one of the first emotional reactions he'd spotted since meeting her. But everyone ended up agreeing that the boys took priority, even Gwen.

The door opened and Sylvia entered the room with a tall demon behind her. Boris stood, as did Misha, as if he knew whoever this demon was could impact his sons.

"This is Nolar," Sylvia said. "Galim called and explained about the twins. I think Nolar can help."

"I'm Abstatholm."

Everyone else pushed back their chairs and stood.

Sylvia stepped in front of Nolar, as if the small human elder could protect him. "I told him he would not be punished for coming here. He could have continued hiding, but instead he wants to help."

"How do we know he isn't behind all of this?" Misha said. "That he didn't do something to my sons?"

Sylvia shook her head. "I've known him for years. He can be trusted."

"Did you know he was Abstatholm?"

"No, but can you blame him for keeping it a secret?"

Nolar spoke up. "I understand your concern. The Abstatholm are looked at poorly on earth. But I did not participate in bringing other demons to earth to force them into servitude. I came here on my own to live."

"He's been helping me acclimate the other demons to earth for years," Sylvia said.

"We can talk about what would happen. I'll explain how I can help your boys open the portal."

"Can they be hurt doing it?" Misha said.

"Nothing is absolute, but from what Sylvia explained to me, I think their issue is not knowing what to do with their massive amounts of energy, and it has thrown the order out of balance."

Misha approached the demon and stared at him for a drawn-out moment. "Make no mistake. If you hurt my sons, I will end you where you stand."

Nolar simply nodded. "I understand. I would do the same if I were you."

The group sat down slowly, and Nolar explained what needed to happen.

When Nolar finished, Misha stood. "I have to talk to Callie about this first. I'll be back."

Misha left, and silence fell on the room as they all became lost in their own thoughts.

Boris wasn't sure how much time had passed when Misha came back into the room with Callie and both boys. When the boys saw Nolar, they sidled closer to Misha's legs, half hiding behind them.

"Hello, boys. I'm Nolar. I understand your powers have started showing themselves."

Matty blinked as a tear ran down his small face. "We hurt Marrick and Sam."

Boris's heart ached for his grandsons. It was a big burden for a small boy.

Nolar knelt down. "You didn't do it on purpose. It was an accident. You didn't know you could create a portal. I'm here to help you bring them home again. Will you let me help you?"

They nodded before stepping out from behind Misha's legs.

"We need everyone to give us some space." He nodded to Misha. "You can stay close by. Bring the ball over here, too."

They had agreed to send something through the portal first before letting Marrick and Sam attempt to come back. With the exception of Misha and Naya and Sabrina, they had also agreed to leave the room so as not to distract the twins. Boris held his arms out, directing everyone out of the room as he looked back over his shoulder.

Nolar continued. "I need you two to face each other and hold hands."

The boys turned and did what he asked.

"Good. Now I want you to close your eyes and listen very carefully to my voice."

Boris left the room and closed the door, hoping the Fates would be on their side today.

Marrick sat down next to Sam on one of the felled tree trunks scattered outside the hut as makeshift seats.

"They're going to try to open the portal," Marrick said.

Sam's breath caught. They had spent time earlier talking to Tarat who, after his initial shock upon learning the Abstatholm responsible were twins who were children, made some suggestions that Marrick communicated to Naya.

"Are they sure?"

"They have an Abstatholm who has come forward and is helping the twins."

"How will they find us?" Sam asked, trying to sound calm.

"The portal should lock on to my device. They're going to throw something through the portal first to see if it comes through." He sighed before turning to her. "We need to talk, Sam."

Now? What was so important that they needed to talk now? Sam could barely concentrate for wondering if they would be on earth soon. If she would see her mother again.

"I don't think you should go through the portal."

She couldn't have heard him correctly.

When she didn't respond immediately, he kept talking. "We don't know what will happen when the portal is formed. It could still be unstable and not safe."

"That's why they're sending something through first."

"An inanimate object. Not a living being."

"But you're going to enter it, right?" Although she already knew the answer.

"Yes."

"Because you're willing to sacrifice yourself."

"I have pledged to help the demons on this world go to earth to start a better life if they choose to."

"You also pledged to get me home," she snapped.

He flinched at her sharp words.

"I did. But you should wait until I can confirm the portal is stable. You'll be safe here in the Kelmar village. I've spoken to Saboll."

Her logical self understood what he was saying. But her emotional self wasn't sold on it.

She and Marrick were in this together and he was going to leave her here? What if she was never able to travel to earth again? She'd thought about the possibility last night as she lay in the cot. And while the thought of them being stuck in the realm scared her to a certain extent—especially the idea of never seeing her mother again—she found comfort in being there with Marrick.

He was special, and the more time she spent with him, the more he invaded her thoughts and, dare she say, maybe her heart? And that kiss. How could a simple—*not* so simple—kiss shake the very earth under her feet? Her world didn't allow for long-term, but with him she was considering it.

But if she was trapped in the realm without him? She didn't need to take her pulse to know it was racing.

"I want to go with you."

"I understand, but I'm asking you to please let me go through first."

She nodded, very reluctantly. Marrick said his goodbyes to Saboll and Tarat and they walked away from the village and into a clearing to wait for the portal.

The air shimmered, and after a few seconds something flew out from the middle of the portal, hit the ground, and rolled to a stop in front of Sam and Marrick. It was a baseball.

Marrick closed his eyes for a moment. He must be telling Naya the ball came through.

He looked at her. "I'll be back for you, Sam, I swear."

And then he entered the portal and left her.

Sam's two selves launched a full-out war in her brain. Apparently her emotional self kicked logical self's ass, because she ran toward the light and flung herself at Marrick, latching onto his back as they were both sucked into the portal.

CHAPTER 24

Marrick felt arms grab him around the waist as the portal yanked him into the vortex. This female! He gripped her hands to make sure she didn't let go while they tumbled through the darkness, trying to drag air into their lungs.

Just when it felt like it was too much, he stumbled into the Shamat meeting hall. Sam was still clinging to him, and he pulled her against his side as soon as she loosened her arms.

Misha held his finger up to his mouth and beckoned for them to move away from the portal.

A large Kelmar knelt by the boys, speaking quietly to them. After a moment, the portal closed.

Marrick grabbed Sam's shoulders and spun her to face him. "You don't listen."

"Nope," she replied, her eyes dancing. "You promised you'd never leave me."

He hugged her to his chest with his chin resting on the top of her head as he breathed in her scent. She hugged him tight, and he realized he was still in his demon form and she was clinging to him.

Naya hurried over. "Are you both okay?"

"Yes." He held Sam at arms' length. "You?"

"Yes."

He turned to the boys, who Misha had grabbed and held in his arms. Sabrina lifted her hands over both their heads and looked like she was using her healing senses to make sure they were unhurt.

After a moment she smiled. "I think you two are going to be just fine."

"Thank you, Matty and Luke, for bringing us home," Sam said.

"Yes, you were very brave," Marrick added.

"Yes, they were," Misha said.

Marrick bowed his head to the Kelmar. "I thank you as well for helping."

"There are a bunch of people out in the hall who want to see you, but we're going to keep this reunion short until I can check you both," Sabrina said.

Naya opened the door, and a crowd rushed into the room behind a wall of cheers. Callie ran over to the boys and started kissing them all over their faces, making them giggle.

But as soon as a petite, blond female walked into the room with Irina, Sam gasped. This must be Sam's mother. Sam had her eyes. And the female looked at her daughter while she headed toward them from across the room, and then at Marrick, her eyes pausing for a moment on his hand. The hand still wrapped around Sam's.

He let her go when Sam lurched forward and almost fell into her mother's arms.

"It's so good to see you, sweetheart. I'm so happy you're safe," the woman said in a soft voice.

Marrick missed what else she said when Irina and Boris stepped up between them and Irina patted his arm. "Welcome back, Marrick!"

Boris reached out a hand and grasped Marrick's forearm. After that, it was a rush of backslaps and "welcome backs" from the group surrounding both him and Sam.

In the midst of all this, Sabrina clapped her hands. "Okay, everyone, we can continue this celebration after I've had a chance to check Marrick and Sam at the hospital. Let's move this across the street."

Marrick turned into his human self before they went outside.

Sam was in front of him with her mother on one side and Irina on the other, while Boris walked alongside him.

Followed by Sabrina, who had stayed behind a couple of seconds to convince the rest of the group to wait in the conference room, promising she'd update them as soon Marrick and Sam had been examined.

As soon as they entered the main reception area, Sam said, "Check Marrick first."

"Check Sam first," Marrick said at the same time.

Sam's expression took on the stubborn glint he was getting to know so well, while she started to explain triage to Marrick who, in her opinion, was the bigger concern due to his medical history.

He put his hands on her shoulders. "Samantha, please let Sabrina look at you first."

She sighed and followed Sabrina into an exam room. Marrick turned and found Gwen watching him. Her face was guarded, but he could sense curiosity and relief.

"It's nice to meet you, Marrick. I'm Gwen. Thank you for taking care of Sam."

"We took care of each other. Sam wouldn't have it any other way."

Gwen actually laughed. "You know my daughter well. She can be stubborn. I don't know where she could have inherited that trait."

Boris coughed into his hand.

Her eyebrows rose. "Are you okay?"

"Yes," Boris responded with a smile.

Interesting. Marrick glanced over to see Irina watching the interchange with a grin. He didn't need to read her emotions to know she was plotting something.

A few minutes later Sam and Sabrina rejoined the group.

"Everything is fine," Sam said. "Your turn now."

Marrick followed Sabrina back into the room and sat on the table while she closed the door.

"I'm surprised Sam didn't insist on staying here."

"She did. But I told her I want to examine you alone."

"Why?"

"Because I want you to be honest about how you're feeling, and I don't know if you would be with Sam in the room."

His head tilted slightly before he could stop himself, but she really was an unusual female, and he couldn't sense any emotions from her at all.

She continued speaking as if the head tilt was a question. "I'm a Succubus demon."

Marrick sat up straighter.

"It means I can sense all different types of connections. Or maybe the better word is 'attractions.' You and Sam share some strong chemistry, and I think you feel the need to protect Sam from the truth. So I'm going to ask you, and I want you to be honest. How are you feeling?"

He thought for a moment before responding. "I actually feel pretty good right now. Better. Just a little tired."

"Tired is to be expected after what you two have been through." She held her hands above his head and then moved them to hover over his chest for a minute.

He held his breath until she opened her eyes and smiled at him. "Your energy feels normal again, so I assume bringing you back through the portal must have stabilized it. I still want to do some blood work and check a couple of other things as well."

He nodded and she began her tests.

Sam walked down the hall, turned around, and walked back for the umpteenth time, pausing, as usual, to stare at the closed exam room door.

"Sam, you're pacing."

"I'm not pacing."

Her mother crossed her arms and gave her The Look.

Sam came to a stop. "Okay. Sorry."

"He'll be fine."

"You don't know that."

"I'm confident that you, Sabrina, and this clan will take good care of Marrick."

Sam gave her a teary smile. "I'm so happy to see you, Mom." Then she took a step closer and lowered her voice—after checking to make sure Boris and Irina were still talking farther down the hall. "But you shouldn't be here."

"If you think I was going to stay away when you weren't answering my calls, you don't know me as well as you always proclaim you do."

Sam sighed. "I know you. When I told Marrick to tell Naya you needed to leave, he asked me if I thought you would really leave. And I said no."

"You told Marrick about me?"

Sam bit her lip. "More than I probably should have. But I didn't know if we would ever get back to earth again. And I was worried about you."

"It's okay. I want you to be able to confide in someone. You and Marrick seem to be close."

Sam could feel her face heat. "We got sucked through a portal into several different worlds and had to rely on each other to survive."

Her mom rolled her eyes at her. "Of course, it was all about survival."

Sam knew that tone all too well. "Mom."

"What, sweetheart?" Her smile grew.

"Don't change the subject. It isn't safe here. As soon as I know Marrick's okay, it's time for us to leave." But even as she said it, her heart protested.

Gwen's grin faded. "You've been accepted into this clan with open arms. Why would you want to leave?"

"Because you can't stay here. Misha is part of the BSR, and his teammates are here all the time. What if someone recognizes you? Boris is on the Demon Council and deals with the leaders. It's too dangerous here for you."

"Which doesn't mean you can't stay here."

What was her mother talking about? Before Sam could argue with her, the door opened and Sabrina came out.

"He's okay...good, actually. He's finishing getting dressed."

"Really?"

"His energy is almost back to normal, as are his blood pressure and pulse. I took some blood and did a couple of other tests just to be cautious, but he should be fine."

Sam could breathe again.

Marrick joined them in the hallway. "There's the smile I wanted to see. I told Sabrina to come out in the hall and tell you so you wouldn't barge into the room and demand answers."

Her mother had the audacity to laugh.

"Hey!"

"I'm sorry, Daughter, but he has you pegged."

"I'm not *that* bad."

Gwen shook her head. "When it comes to someone you care about, you're ferocious."

Sam's face heated again before she looked at Marrick, who gave her a wicked grin.

A voice spoke behind her. "I take it from the smiles that you both received a clean bill of health?"

Sam turned to find Boris standing in the hall.

"Yes," Marrick said. "What about the portal?"

"Naya was able to open the portal, as was Krell in the realm. It appears the issue has been resolved."

"And the boys are okay?" Sam asked.

"Yes. And Nolar has volunteered to help them learn about their powers to prevent something like this from happening again."

Boris took a couple of steps closer. "You shouldn't be surprised to learn that Irina has decided to throw an impromptu celebration with you two and the twins as the guests of honor. If you three are up to it, we're going to have some food over in the community center. I promise I won't let them keep you long, since I'm sure you're exhausted."

Marrick looked at Sam, who nodded. Sam looked at her mother, who also nodded.

Boris rubbed his hands together. "Excellent! Sabrina, will you be joining us?"

"In a few minutes."

Sam and Marrick walked side by side back to the community center, followed by Boris and Gwen. As happy as Sam was now that they'd returned to earth and Marrick was well again, the idea of leaving hurt her heart.

Marrick glanced over at her several times during their walk to the community center. He was probably picking up on her emotions. She needed to talk to him, but not with her mother and Boris watching and listening. She had to explain to him why she was leaving.

But he had his own job to do in the realm. He would understand.

As soon as they entered the meeting room in the community center, they were greeted by a cheer. The twins ran to them and grabbed onto Marrick and Sam's legs.

Sam laughed out loud as she looked over at Marrick. She had never felt like she belonged before.

Just in time to leave it all behind.

CHAPTER 25

Gwen was astonished. This was what she'd always wanted for her daughter. A clan to call her own, and hopefully a mate to spend her life with. The way Sam and Marrick were looking at each other, she was getting her wish.

She just needed to convince her daughter she belonged here. And she wasn't sure how she was going to do it without Sam figuring out what she was up to. It was time for Gwen to face down her past. And as long as Sam was happy and loved, she could do it.

The group swarmed around Marrick and Sam again until Gwen finally made her way over to her daughter and pulled her into her arms, holding on with all her strength.

Gwen watched over Sam's shoulder while Misha joined his father and whispered in his ear.

Boris's expression changed at his son's words. He turned his gaze on her. She ran her hand over Sam's hair to ground herself for a few moments instead of running for the door.

He knew who she was.

But there would be no more running from her past, or from the look in his eyes.

Gwen released her daughter and backed up so Sam could talk to her friends. Then she approached Boris and stopped in front of him.

"Follow me," Boris said.

She followed him out of the room and down a short hallway into his office. She glanced around this time at the shelves to the side containing books and various pictures of Boris's family.

Gwen looked at the pictures. "I'm surprised you haven't summoned a guard."

"Should I?"

She turned to him. "I knew he'd figure it out eventually."

"If Misha hadn't been so upset about what was happening with his sons, he probably would have figured it out sooner. So you're not going to deny it?"

"I'm not going to deny I'm wanted by the Pavel, but I didn't do what they're accusing me of."

"You didn't murder their leader?"

"I did not."

Boris frowned. "It's been a while, but if I remember the story, you worked as a servant for Augustus and killed him by surprise."

She blew out a harsh breath. "Right. A Dalmot demon took down one of the most powerful Pavel living at the time. Does that make any sense to you?"

"You don't need to be powerful if you gained his trust. Stealth can work in your favor as well."

"For what reason? What was my motive, exactly?"

"Why don't you tell me what happened, then?"

"Why?" Gwen asked.

"Because I can't help you if you don't tell me the truth. How did you come to work for Augustus?"

Gwen crossed her arms, mostly since she didn't know what to do with her hands—or her arms, for that matter. She hadn't told anyone her story...her truth...in more than a hundred years. But he said he was willing to help her. If he was going to trust her, shouldn't she do the same?

"My mate Jonathan and I came from a small Dalmot clan in England. Jonathan was a warrior for hire who was part of the Pavel army during the last demon border wars, and while he was on the battlefield, I started working in the kitchen at Augustus's estate house. Jonathan was killed in a skirmish, and I found out I was pregnant a few months later."

She thought back to that time. "I would take food to Augustus, and when he noticed I was with child, he asked about my mate, and I told him Jonathan had been killed. After that, Augustus ordered me to deliver his food nightly, and after I had Sam, he had me assigned as his personal servant."

She looked up at Boris. "There was never anything between Augustus and me other than friendship. He had lost his wife and daughter to a terrible disease centuries earlier, and he took a shine to the two of us, especially Sam. He loved Sam to pieces, but didn't let anyone know it for fear she would be used against him. The night he was..." She choked on the words even after all this time.

After a couple of deep breaths, she continued. "I was working in the kitchen, preparing a special meal and Augustus was in his private quarters preparing for a dance that night while Sam played in the dressing room with her dolls."

"Augustus didn't mind Sam being there?"

"He acted like he did, but it was all bluster. He actually liked Sam being around as long as she behaved herself, especially if he had guests."

"When I got back to the rooms, I found Augustus on the floor with a fatal wound to the chest." The words resurrected her panic as if it were happening now. She closed her eyes for a moment before continuing.

"Where was Sam?"

"There was a cupboard in the dressing room where Sam played hide-and-seek. I found her inside the space, curled in a tight ball and clutching the doll Augustus had given her. She had blood on her hands, and she kept opening her mouth as if to scream, but no sound came out." Gwen cleared her throat. "I checked her over to see if she was hurt, and quickly saw the blood wasn't hers. I gathered her into my arms and ran down the back stairs of the house and through the courtyard into the night."

"Why did you run and not go to the authorities?"

She swallowed. "How could I not run? I had no idea who had killed him, and Sam had been in the room. Within hours they declared I was involved with the murder. Drawings were distributed around the city. There would be no fair trial for me. I would have been executed. Who would have taken care of my daughter? A daughter who was completely unable to talk about whatever she'd witnessed that night?

"I ran as far and as fast as I could. Sam didn't talk for years, except when she had nightmares. Then she would scream until she finally fell into an exhausted sleep, clinging to her doll as if it was a lifeline. I finally found a healer who was able to lock away her memories of the night so she could begin to function again."

Boris frowned slightly.

"I know it wasn't the best way, but I'd already worked with several healers, and none could get Sam to talk at all, let alone talk about what had happened. After the memories were suppressed, she opened her eyes and said my name. It was...and still is...the most glorious thing I've ever heard.

"After that, a small village clan let us live with them for a few years. When Sam turned eleven, I actually left her with one of the females who became a dear friend to me. I was too scared to travel with Sam in case I was captured. The best thing I could do was stay far, far away and let my daughter have a fresh start."

"When Sam turned sixteen, I came back to see her. She informed me that if I tried to leave her again, she would follow me. That we belonged together."

"And you've been on the run ever since?"

"Yes. We've split up for a while from time to time, for Sam's safety, but she always insists we get back together again."

"And that's why Sam came here."

"Yes."

"You had to know there's a large Pavel clan here in Cleveland. Why would Sam choose to come here?"

"She didn't. I sent her."

Boris couldn't have heard her right. "What?"

"I found the job for Sam and contacted Irina, pretending to be Sam. Once I had the interview set up, I packed Sam's bag and handed her a bus ticket."

What was this female playing at? "Why?"

"We've been on the run for more than a hundred and fifty years, and knowing your enemy is the best way to survive. I sent her here because your clan is the best defense against the Pavel. If anyone can stand up against them, it's you.

"I wanted Sam to be part of a clan, a family. She's never had that kind of stability and safety in her life, and I want her to feel—and be—protected and loved. And based on what I've learned about your clan, you take in outsiders as part of your own. Hell, you're leading the fight to bring the realm demons here. You are the perfect fit for my daughter."

She stood taller when she finished her speech, and he stared at her.

He had always thought the saying "a lightbulb went off" was a bit over the top, but in that moment it was exactly what happened to him.

"You're turning yourself in? Sacrificing yourself?"

She looked away for just a moment before she turned back to him with her mask securely fastened over her emotions. "Don't make me sound heroic. I'm sick of running. Josiah Akers has been in China for more than a month now. The Pavel leader rarely leaves the States, so this was my chance to get as far away from Sam as I could when I turned myself in."

"You're doing this so your daughter can have a normal life."

She glanced at the pictures of his family he had on his bookcase. "I think you understand."

He did, damn it. But knowing didn't make this whole situation any less awful.

Boris's phone beeped and he ignored it. Then it beeped again and again.

"You better get that. It sounds important."

He pulled the phone out of his pocket and read the first message, and then the next. He swore in Russian. Why were the Fates toying with them?

"I don't know what you said, but I don't think it was a very nice word."

"An emergency Council meeting has been called. Akers wants a report of what happened. He'll probably try to close down the immigration project, declaring it is too dangerous for everyone involved."

"He's back in town?"

"Not yet, but he wants to deal with what he's calling an 'out-of-control situation.'"

"Well, now you can hand me over to him instead of me going to China."

"Do you think that's what I want to do? Hand you over?"

"No, which is why I know I made the right choice sending Sam here. But you can't just let me go. If the truth gets out, you'll lose credibility with the Council, and Akers will have his way. The immigration can't afford that. My arrest will probably distract him for a while so he doesn't try to shut the immigration down."

"Let's talk to Misha and his teammates. We can try to do something."

Her resigned smile soured his stomach. "Even you won't be able to save me."

"You sent Sam here because of this clan, so don't discount us now. I'm going to get Misha and his team, and we're going to talk this through."

She nodded. "Will you promise me one thing?"

"What?"

"Will you take care of Sam for me?"

This female had been fighting for a hundred and fifty years, and she was going to give up now? He took a breath. But she wasn't giving up, she was changing the future for her daughter. "Of course I'll take care of Sam, if she'll let me."

Gwen frowned. "What do you mean?"

"I don't know whether Sam will want anything to do with me, or this clan, if I turn you over to the Pavel."

CHAPTER 26

Marrick watched Sam from across the room while she talked to Aleksei and Irina. Aleksei said something that made Irina burst out laughing and Sam smiled, but didn't join in their revelry.

Something was wrong. Being in a room with a crowd could overwhelm Marrick's empathic ability, so he'd learned how to hold others' emotions at bay.

But he wasn't pushing Sam's emotions away. Far from it. He could sense relief from her, and happiness, even if it was muted. What concerned him was the growing sadness he felt building in her. Why was she sad?

She looked around the room as if searching for someone, and anxiety began to invade her emotions as well.

Marrick glanced around the room. Sam's mother was missing and, now that he was paying attention, he noticed Misha, Kyle, and the rest of the BSR team were gone as well.

He wanted to go straight over and ask her what was wrong, but she wouldn't appreciate him confronting her in front of the clan. As soon as he could get her alone, though, she would answer his questions.

Naya joined him, looking very cheerful. "I'm glad you're okay, my friend."

"So you told me earlier."

"That doesn't mean I can't say it again."

She followed his gaze, turning to study Sam. "You two have grown close."

He finally managed to wrestle his attention away from Sam and looked at his sister, not by blood, but by friendship. "Yes."

Her eyes flared at his acquiescence. "I'm glad you were honest. Otherwise we would have spent a lot of back and forth trying to get the truth out of you."

Marrick shook his head and sighed. "You've been spending too much time with Irina and Kyle."

Naya laughed. "They're family. As are you."

Marrick saw Misha enter the room and say something to Aleksei. Aleksei nodded and followed his brother out of the room.

"Something is wrong," Marrick said.

Naya frowned. "You can feel something?"

"No, but the BSR team is gone, and Misha just came for Aleksei."

A few seconds later Sam headed out the same door Misha and Aleksei had left through. "Excuse me."

He hurried into the hall. "Sam!"

She looked over her shoulder, fear radiating off her in waves. "I'm going to find my mom."

"Let me go with you."

They headed down the hall where offices were located, and heard a low murmur of voices, confirming they were going in the right direction.

Sam sped up, and before he could tell her to wait, she shoved open the office door. Aleksei, Boris, and the BSR team were in the room with Gwen standing in the middle of the group.

"Mom? What's going on?"

The group stood in silence for a moment and Sam looked at her mother's face. Sam's fear blossomed into terror.

"No!" She turned to Boris. "You can't turn her over. You can't!"

"Sweetheart," Gwen said.

"No! We'll leave. Let us leave. You'll never see us again."

Sam's words tore into Marrick's guts like a blade.

"We're trying to figure out how to defend her," Boris said, his voice rough.

Sam rushed over to Boris. "Don't do this."

"Sam!" Gwen said. "It's too late. They have to turn me over or it could jeopardize the immigration."

"They're going to sacrifice you for their cause."

"It was my choice."

Sam spun to face her mother. "What are you talking about?"

"Even if they hadn't figured out who I am, this would have happened anyway. I was already planning to turn myself in to the Pavel."

Marrick had a hard time taking a full breath, and he realized he was experiencing what Sam was. Anger, fear, and betrayal were warring within her as she stared at her mother.

"That's why you said earlier that I could stay here. You planned on leaving me here for good. We promised we would always stay together. Always!"

"To what end, Sam? To spend your entire life on the run? To never experience belonging somewhere? To never have love or a family? I can't bring myself to keep doing that to you."

"*You* are my family. You're enough for me."

Gwen closed her eyes for a moment before she opened them again and rested her hands on her daughter's shoulders. "You're lying to me, and to yourself. I see the way you are here. This is where you need to be. I will not let you sacrifice your happiness for me."

"But you can sacrifice yourself for me?"

"Damn straight. I'm. Your. Mother. When I first felt you flutter in my belly, I loved you, and when I first held you in my arms, I pledged I would do everything in my power to protect you. I thought I was protecting you while we hid away from the world. But as the decades passed, I realized this life isn't protection, and it's suffocating you."

"So you made the decision without talking to me."

"You wouldn't have let me do it, Sam. You would have fought me, and I couldn't risk you doing something that would endanger you. That would hurt you."

A tear trickled down Sam's cheek. "Except you're hurting me now. And all your scheming to find me a family isn't going to work." She looked around at the faces in the room. "If you turn her in, I won't stay here. I won't be a part of this clan."

She ran out of the room.

"Sam!" Gwen called after her.

"I'll go to her," Marrick said.

He found Sam outside the community center, pain spraying off her like a million pinpricks. She doubled over, and Marrick grabbed her before she hit the ground.

He held onto her while she cried, wretched, gut-wrenching sobs. But he couldn't think of a thing to say that would help her feel better.

Her despair had engulfed her like a tide.

All he could do was hold her above the waves so she wasn't sucked under.

Chapter 27

Sam had never been more exhausted in her entire life. She'd sobbed like a baby in Marrick's arms until she couldn't cry another tear.

He didn't try to tell her everything would be okay, which she appreciated. Having his arms around her kept her from falling apart altogether and running until she couldn't run anymore. Wasn't that what she and her mom had been doing for more than a century?

Until her mother decided to stop running.

After Sam pulled herself back together, she spoke to her mother again, this time alone, but it was no good. She'd made up her mind. And as much as Sam loved her mother for her strength and determination, right now she wanted her to back down.

Any minute now the emergency Council meeting about the immigration was scheduled to begin. And of course her mother was preparing to rock that boat—hell, she was going to blow it out of the water.

Her mother told Sam she didn't want her in the meeting room. Sam had simply stared at her, trying to register what she was saying. Something about not exposing her to the Council and keeping her safe, but Sam couldn't see it for anything but a separation.

Her mom was breaking away from her now, as if Sam would, or could, simply move on, and magically everything would be normal.

Nothing would ever be normal again.

Even after her first real shower in weeks and a change of clothes, she still felt helpless and sad. And she stood in the middle of Irina's guest room at a loss. What was she supposed to do next?

Marrick had wanted to stay with her, but he needed to go to the meeting to report what happened with the portal, and she'd insisted he go.

As much as her mother wanted her to cut ties, she wouldn't—couldn't—do it. If her mom was going to turn herself over to the Pavel leader, shouldn't Sam be there to support her?

Her breath hitched. *Pull it together.* She opened the door quietly, in case Irina was somewhere in the house, because she'd probably try to stop her from going to the meeting.

Sam made it to the community center and down the hall faster than she wanted to, and paused outside the room to listen. She peeked through the thin window in the door. She was getting too adept at eavesdropping.

Boris brought the meeting to order. He and Aleksei explained how the portal was working again and had been stabilized.

"And how exactly was the portal impacted?" one of the leaders asked.

Before Boris could answer them, Sam's mother spoke up. "I think the Shamat leader has something else important to bring to your attention."

"What the hell is the meaning of this!" a male bellowed.

"I take it you know who I am, Josiah," Gwen said.

"There isn't a Pavel alive who doesn't have the drawing of your likeness memorized. You murdered our leader!" Akers shouted.

"Why is she in the Shamat compound?" another leader demanded.

"She turned herself in to a neutral party," Boris said.

"I will have guards there in less than an hour to take her into custody," Akers said.

"No," Boris said.

"No? You don't get to tell me no, Shamat."

In spite of her intention to stand with her mom, Sam couldn't get herself to open the door.

What was it about the Pavel leader's voice that wrapped icy tentacles around her spine? She wanted to run, as fast as she could, and far, far away.

She could see Boris's profile through the window in the door and he smiled. "But I can. According to the Demon Rights Charter, if a demon is concerned about their safety while in custody, they are allowed to request protection from another clan. She will remain incarcerated here throughout her trial."

"I'm leaving China as soon as my jet gains clearance. In the meantime, I will be sending my security to ensure she remains incarcerated."

Sam's hand shook as she reached for the door and opened it. She had come here to be with her mom, not hide in the hallway.

She pushed open the door and walked in to see her mother standing next to Boris in front of a computer screen.

The tension was as thick as pudding in the room, the same feeling as when she traveled through the portal and the air pushed in from all sides. Sam looked up at the screen on the wall to see the faces of the leaders in squares, like the last meeting. She searched out Josiah Akers to find out what he looked like, even though her nerves were screeching along her skin like nails on a chalkboard.

When she finally saw Akers, her muscles spasmed and something split inside her. Her vision grayed, and when it cleared again, she was watching the scene from above, as if her consciousness left her body and floated near the ceiling. She watched her mother turn, and Marrick sprinting across the room toward her, and heard the screaming.

A wounded animal sound she realized only belatedly was coming from her as it blasted through her throat like fire. And she couldn't stop.

A familiar but sickening metallic scent burned her nose, and she looked down at her blood-covered hands. She had to get away. To hide, like Augustus told her. She should have listened. Why didn't she listen?

Time to hide. The keening continued, and she finally slipped away into darkness.

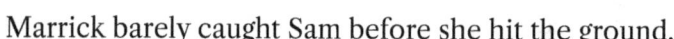

Marrick barely caught Sam before she hit the ground.

He couldn't breathe.

Something was terribly wrong.

Sam's emotions were all over the place, as if they'd splintered. He picked her up, ignoring the yells coming from the Council leaders and everyone else in the room, and sprinted out the door and down the hallway. He turned and used his back to slam into the bar on the door, pushing it open and racing across the lawn and street and into the hospital.

The receptionist took one look at him and hit a button on her desk that set an alarm ringing. Healers came running from all directions, including Sabrina.

"Follow me," she said as they hurried into a room.

He lay Sam down on the bed with wheels and people flocked around her.

"Tell me what happened," Sabrina said.

"She was in the meeting with the Demon Council, and her mother had just turned herself into the Pavel. Sam started screaming and then collapsed."

"No one touched her or attacked her?"

"No. But it's bad, Sabrina. Her emotions. It's like something tore apart inside her."

Sabrina nodded and then turned her attention to the other people in the room as they started doing tests on Sam and using words he didn't understand.

Sabrina made him wait in the hall, but he remained right next to the closed door. He'd never been so scared in his life. Not when facing down a gang of angry realm demons or fighting for his life. Sam had to be okay.

He wasn't sure how long he'd been waiting in the hall, listening, when Gwen and Naya rushed toward him.

"How is she?" Gwen asked.

"I don't know. They haven't told me anything. Is the meeting still happening?"

Naya frowned. "If you can call it that. Boris and Aleksei finally got everyone to stop yelling. They're talking about how Gwen's trial will be held. The only reason we're here is because I took Gwen into custody and said I was taking her to a detention cell."

"At least my arrest has distracted the Council from talking about the immigration."

The door opened and Sabrina came out.

"How is she?" Gwen and Marrick asked at the same time.

Sabrina gestured for them to follow her across the hall into an empty room.

"We're still running tests, and I've also been using my healing senses. From what I can tell so far, it doesn't appear to be physical. It's more fundamental. It's her emotions, her psyche. Something triggered this, and it's overloaded her. She isn't mentally here with us now. Can you tell me if something like this has happened before with Sam?"

Gwen nodded while tears coursed down her face. She explained about the murder and what Sam was like when she found her afterward.

Marrick wanted to scream, to rail against the bastards who had made these two women run for their lives for more than a hundred years.

Gwen scrubbed her hands over her face. "Finally seeing me arrested must have pushed her too far. Brought back the memories that were suppressed more than a hundred years ago."

Sabrina rested her hand on Gwen's arm.

"Can I see her?" Gwen asked.

"Give me a few minutes to finish the tests." Sabrina went back into the room and shut the door.

Marrick stared across the hall at the closed door. A phone rang and he turned. Naya pulled out her cell phone and answered it. "Hold on a second." She put the phone down by her thigh. "I'm going to take this down the hall. I'll be back."

"Thank you, Marrick."

He turned to Gwen. "I've done nothing."

"When Sam started screaming, your first reaction was to get to her, everyone else be damned. You had her at the hospital before the rest of us even registered what was going on."

"Sam is still suffering," he said.

Gwen blew out a hard breath. "And that's on me. If I hadn't decided to turn myself in, none of this would have happened."

"Based on what you described, Sam's memories would have come to the surface eventually. That much pain can't remain buried forever."

"Well, now I won't be able to protect Sam." She gazed up at him, as if trying to make a decision, before she finally spoke again. "I see the way you look at my daughter, Marrick. You care for her. Hell, you may even love her."

He gaped at her.

"You don't have to say anything right now. I'm not the first one you should say it to, anyway. But I need your help to protect Sam."

"Anything," he said, without hesitation.

"If the Pavel try to take her into custody, we can't let it happen."

"Why would they do that? She was a child when Augustus was killed."

"Because of the severity of this crime, they may try to punish my immediate family members. Sam could be imprisoned."

The thought of Sam being locked away robbed him of breath. "I'll protect her."

Gwen stood and looked out the door before she turned back to him. "You can take her back to the realm with you."

"She's hurt. She needs to be in the hospital."

Gwen blinked shiny eyes. "If Josiah Akers comes after her, there's nowhere on earth where she'll be safe. And I believe if anyone can get through to her, you can."

"What makes you think so?"

"Because I've heard my daughter's voice when she speaks of you, and have seen what she will do to protect you. Sam doesn't trust easily, which is my fault. So when I tell you she cares for you, it's not to be taken lightly."

He nodded.

"Will you do this for Sam?"

"I will watch over her with my life."

A subtle expression flickered across Gwen's face. "No wonder Sam cares for you."

Marrick didn't have a chance to respond before Sabrina appeared in the doorway. "You can see her for a few moments."

Marrick's breathing sped up as they crossed the hall. Sam was lying on her side with her legs pulled up. Machines behind her beeped, and strange lines appeared on the front of a box with a shiny cover.

Gwen rounded the bed and placed her hand on Sam's shoulder. "Is she in pain?" she asked in a soft voice.

Sabrina shook her head. "Nothing physical. She won't respond to any of us. Try and talk to her."

Gwen leaned over and spoke quietly in Sam's ear. Sam didn't react or move. After a few minutes, Gwen stood up.

Naya appeared in the doorway, scowling. "The Pavel who are to supervise your incarceration have arrived. I'm sorry, but we've got to take you to the cell."

"Okay." Gwen leaned down and kissed Sam on the top of her head before walking around the bed. She stopped in front of Marrick. "You'll take care of her for me?"

"Absolutely."

Naya looked between Marrick and Gwen before beckoning for Gwen to come with her.

Gwen turned to Sabrina. "Since I won't be easily available to discuss things about Sam, Marrick will serve as my proxy."

Sabrina nodded. "Of course."

Gwen and Naya left the room, and Marrick hurried over to Sam and cradled her hand in both of his.

"How are you doing?" Sabrina asked.

"I'm fine," he said quickly.

She gazed at him for a moment before looking at the jumping lines on the shiny boxes. "I'm going to move Sam to a hospital room. She'll be more comfortable, and there'll be room for you as well, since I assume you plan to stay with her."

He nodded, and she left the room.

Marrick ran his hand over Sam's head, brushing her hair back from her face. "I'm here, Sam. You're safe. I won't let any harm come to you."

But he had, hadn't he? Could he have foreseen this? Protected her from fear and pain so powerful they stripped her of consciousness?

Sam's mother trusted him to protect her. And he would do anything for this female in front of him.

He straightened, shocked by the intensity of emotions surging through him. And it was the intensity that made him pause. He had locked his emotions away for so long, he wasn't sure if he would ever truly feel again.

Until Sam burst into his life. And he realized feelings weren't the enemy. The true enemy was living a half-life. And Sam would never let him settle for that. She had saved him.

Now it was his turn to save her.

CHAPTER 28

Marrick remained in the hospital room that, as the hours ticked on, felt more and more like a cell.

He hadn't left Sam's side in thirty-six hours. Between the hospital staff and the rest of the clan checking on them, he also hadn't been alone long enough to let his thoughts or despair drown him.

But as he gazed down at Sam—who hadn't moved, regardless of who spoke to her or what they did to her—his emotions suffocated him. She didn't even flinch when Sabrina examined her or had more blood taken. How much blood could they possibly need from such a small female?

Over the past few hours, a plan had emerged. He needed to tell the others about his idea, since he didn't want to risk it alone, so he had asked Naya to gather those he needed to "put this idea in motion," as the earthers would say.

At a light knock on the door, he turned to greet Irina. Instead of hurrying over to Sam, she rested both her hands on his arms. "I understand you have an idea to help our Sam."

He nodded, a little breathless about her use of the word *our*.

She patted him. "I'm here to stay with Sam while you discuss this with the others."

"Thank you."

He went over to Sam and rested his hand on her arm while he leaned close to her ear. "I'll be back shortly, Sam. We're going to make you better soon."

Fates willing.

In the hall he found Naya waiting for him, and they fell in step as they walked across the street. Apparently Naya didn't expect him to talk, which he appreciated, since he was still organizing his thoughts around the best way to present this to the group.

When they entered the community center meeting hall, they found Boris, Aleksei, Sabrina, Kyle, and Misha waiting for them.

"Thank you for meeting with me," Marrick said.

"Of course. We'll do whatever we can to help Sam," Boris said.

A few seconds later, the door opened and Sergei rushed in. "Sorry I'm late."

"No problem," Marrick said. "What about Gwen?"

Boris frowned. "I told her we could hold this meeting at the detention center, but she doesn't want the Pavel guards to overhear our discussion. She's very concerned that they'll try to arrest Sam as well."

Kyle leaned forward. "They can't do that, right?"

"There is some precedent, with a crime of this severity, indicating that the accused *and* their family can be punished for it," Aleksei said.

"That's a load of bullshit!" Kyle blurted.

"I couldn't agree more, Kyle," Boris said. "It hasn't been used in over a century. Unfortunately, this crime took place a hundred and fifty years ago, and I wouldn't put it past Akers to try resurrecting it. But first things first. We need to get Sam healthy." Boris turned to Marrick. "What is your plan?"

Marrick sighed. "This isn't common knowledge, but I'm a high-level empath. I can feel emotions from others. I've spent the past day and a half with Sam, trying to figure out what's going on with her."

"Can you sense anything?" Naya asked.

"The problem is, I can sense too much. Her memories triggered emotions that are bombarding her all at once, and constantly. Fear, anger, and sorrow have become terror, hatred, and agony. I think she shut down to protect herself."

"What are you going to do?" Naya asked.

"I'm going to try to strip away the emotions drowning her. If I'm able to do it, maybe she can finally face the memories."

Naya frowned. "What you're really saying is you're going to pull her emotions into yourself. Isn't it dangerous? What if you're overwhelmed by them? Then what?"

"I have to try, Naya. She's not getting any better. What if her body starts to shut down because of this? You'd do the same for Aleksei."

"Yes, I would."

Sabrina spoke up. "And keep in mind that Sam isn't responding to anything we've tried so far, and I don't know how long her body can handle this stress."

Marrick continued. "I would like Naya and Kyle's help as well."

"What do you want us to do?" Kyle asked.

"Kyle, your power is centered on changing memories. Have you ever been able to see memories?"

"Rarely, but it does happen. Are you thinking if I can see her memories, we can talk her out of them?"

"Maybe. Which is where Naya could help with her telepathy. If I can strip away the emotions, maybe you can talk to her."

"I'm willing to try," Naya said.

"What if Lela is also here to give us a boost of power?" Kyle asked.

Marrick nodded. "I had hoped we could include Lela as well."

Sergei frowned. "Lela isn't able to help right now."

Boris rested his hand on his son's arm. "What's wrong with Lela, Son? I'm worried."

Sergei looked over at Sabrina and seemed to make a decision. "This isn't how we wanted to share the news, but I also don't want you to worry. Lela hasn't been feeling well, and Sabrina just confirmed for us that she's pregnant."

Boris gripped his son's arm. "She's okay, Sabrina?"

"Yes. I've just finished telling her to take it easy and not share her energy right now."

Boris embraced his son as congratulations were given. Sergei grinned. "With everything going on, we had decided to wait to tell you all."

"So we move forward with the plan without Lela's help."

"I actually have an idea," Sergei said. "I think Lela could help, but indirectly. Since my power is the ability to mimic other demon powers, I'll mimic Lela's power and help boost your powers as well if I can."

"You don't need to drain her energy to do it, correct?" Marrick said.

"Correct. I don't drain powers when I mimic them. I just need to come into contact with a demon and I can absorb their learned powers."

"Thank you," Marrick said.

"When do you want to do this?" Naya asked.

"When does the trial start?" Marrick asked.

"Tomorrow," Boris said. "Akers arrived home today, and the Council will be here in the morning."

"Then we should try today. I don't want them anywhere near Sam when she's vulnerable."

What he didn't say was, whether or not this worked, he would do whatever it took to keep her from being arrested, even if it meant taking her to the realm.

CHAPTER 29

Marrick gazed down at Sam while Kyle, Naya, Sergei, and Sabrina filed into the room.

Sergei rested his hands on Naya's shoulders for a few seconds before moving to Kyle, and then finally to Marrick. Warmth flowed through Marrick's body, and he nodded to Sergei as the male moved back out of the way and leaned against the wall.

Naya moved to the other side of Sam's bed, and Kyle stationed herself at the foot. Sabrina stood next to the boxes he had learned were called monitors to watch over Sam.

Marrick looked first at Kyle and then Naya before closing his eyes and concentrating on Sam. She was still a jumble of emotions, all tangled together, and smothering her. Marrick reached for one emotion...anger...that squirmed around and tried to avoid him until he was able to latch on to it. When he did, it burned his chest, and he sucked in a breath but continued peeling it away from her, slowly, so as not to shock her.

He moved on to despair, which dumped a horrible, sour taste into his mouth that ran down into his throat and made him cough. He opened his eyes and saw the hand closest to her was glowing as if it was reaching inside her and pulling away the pain.

Marrick? Naya spoke softly in his mind.

I'm okay. It's working, but I have to go slowly.

He went back to pulling away the emotions. Confusion, loneliness, guilt, the list went on, and he absorbed them one by one while they made his stomach twist and his head spin.

There were still some residual emotions, but the one left that he had to remove if they had any hope of reaching Sam: fear.

And the word was a pale descriptor of what continually hammered Sam's psyche. In reality, it was the kind of unadulterated, mindless terror that locked your muscles and stole your breath. He staggered back a step when he attempted to latch on to it. It was so cold it burned him. Strong hands pressed against his back, supporting him as warmth spread through him while Sergei pushed more power into him.

Marrick was finally able to pry the emotion away from her, and he nodded while Sergei helped him sit down next to her, since his legs were no longer steady.

Then he motioned to Naya and Kyle, and they leaned toward the bed, each closing her eyes.

Sabrina then joined them at the bed and held her hands over Sam, concentrating. Marrick prayed the Fates were on their side right now.

After a few minutes, Naya opened her eyes and shook her head. "She won't talk to me."

Marrick's heart pinched. She had to be better. Had to. "Sabrina?"

"Her heart rate and pulse and breathing are much more stable than before. My senses also tell me she's doing better."

"Why isn't she awake, then?" Marrick asked.

Kyle opened her eyes. "I think she's still trying to work something out. It's like she's caught in a memory loop right now."

"What do you mean?" Marrick asked.

"I can see bits and pieces of a memory. I think it's from when she was a child. From the flashes I can make out, I think she's reliving when Augustus was killed."

Marrick attempted to stand, and Sergei reached out and steadied him when he got to his feet. Sabrina went over and held her hands up in front of Marrick.

After a few seconds, she lowered her arms. "I should probably order you to lie down and rest, but I think you'd just ignore me."

"Yes. How do we help her?"

"I think we have helped her. The rest is up to Sam to work out on her own."

Marrick reached for Sam's hand and wrapped his own larger hand around it. She could do this. He had to believe she would be okay, or he would curl up into a ball himself.

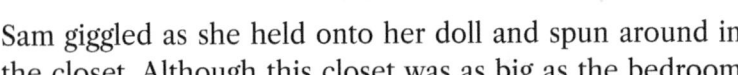

Sam giggled as she held onto her doll and spun around in the closet. Although this closet was as big as the bedroom she shared with her mother.

On the dresser in the closet sat some of Gus's jewelry. She hadn't known males wore jewelry until he showed her.

Sam reached for the shiny metal.

"Don't touch the ring, Samantha," a voice rumbled from behind her.

She jerked her hand back and looked up at him.

"You can look at the watch, but never touch the ring."

She nodded. Grandpa Gus had told her that before. She needed to 'member it. Just like she had to 'member not to call him *grandpa* unless they were alone. "It's pretty."

He put the ring on his finger. "It is, but it's also dangerous. Only I can wear the ring."

"Because you're special."

The frowns around his eyes disappeared. "Yes. So, Samantha, please promise me you won't touch the ring."

"I promise."

He tucked his watch into the front pocket of his vest. "What do you think is taking Gwendolyn so long?"

"Momma said she's making your favorite dinner."

"What is that?"

"Rabbit stew."

"I don't know if rabbit stew is my favorite or your favorite?"

Sam giggled. "Both."

Gus patted her head.

Sam jumped at a bang that came from outside the room. Who was banging on the door? Gus's guards should have stopped them from making such a loud noise.

"Mark, report!"

But his guard didn't answer.

Gus frowned. "Samantha. Climb into the cupboard where you play hide-and-seek. Can you do that for me? And can you be really quiet?"

"Yes."

"Go on, now. Be a good girl and stay in the cupboard until I call for you."

She nodded, climbed inside, and he shut the door behind her. She gasped at the darkness. He had never shut it tight before.

She pushed her bum against the corner and hugged her doll to keep her company. Raised voices made her cower down farther. Gus sounded mad.

Then she heard a loud, scary thump that made her bury her face against her doll's dress. What happened? She heard

Gus cry out in pain, and she slid across the cupboard and pushed open the door just a little bit. Maybe he was hurt and needed help. Momma could help him.

Sam peeked out and didn't see anyone, so she climbed out and tiptoed to the door leading into the sitting room, which was where Gus met with other grown-ups.

Gus was on his knees in front of a large Pavel who held a knife.

"You would do this to me, your own blood?"

"It's time for new leadership."

Gus punched up into the demon's chest and the demon grunted in pain. A circle of red spread across the demon's shirt.

"You will be marked forever as a traitor," Gus said.

Sam scrambled backward and rushed back to her hidey-hole, pulled the door shut, and put her hand over her mouth so her breathing wouldn't sound so loud. So very loud.

She heard another thump and closed her eyes. This was a bad dream. Her momma would wake her up and tell her it was okay.

After a while it was quiet. Where was Gus? Where was her momma? Sam opened the door again and crept out into the room.

Gus was lying on the floor.

She ran over to him and said his name, but he didn't look at her.

She hadn't been a good girl! She wasn't supposed to leave the cupboard, but she did.

Now Gus wouldn't wake up. She pushed on his chest and her hands got wet. Red. So much red. It was like when she fell, but she couldn't stop it from coming out of his chest the way Momma had fixed it when Sam scraped her knee.

Something shiny caught her eye. It was Gus's ring, lying under a chair. The one that made him special. Sam picked up the ring and looked at it. Red stained the metal, and she bit her lip.

Then she heard noise out in the hall and ran back into the closet and into the cupboard, grabbing her doll and hunkering down.

What if someone found out she had his ring? She wasn't supposed to touch the ring.

She pulled up her doll's dress and looked for the frayed space where some of the stuffing had escaped. She pushed the ring into the doll, far down into her tummy, so no one would find it.

She was a bad girl. She should have listened. What if the demon who hurt Gus came looking for her now?

Sam jerked upright.

Hands grasped her shoulders. She batted at the hands and opened her mouth to scream.

"Sam! You're okay. It's Marrick."

She blinked and he came into focus. "Marrick?" She looked around the room. "Where am I?"

"In the hospital. You collapsed two days ago."

Two days? *What?*

Then she remembered. Her mom had turned herself in to the Demon Council and then everything went black. "Where's my mom?"

"She's under arrest." He looked up at the clock on the wall. "Her trial is going to start any minute now."

Sam threw back the covers. "We have to go."

"Wait! Slow down. You just woke up."

"We have to go help her."

Sam attempted to stand, but the room whirled.

Marrick helped her back onto the bed. "You haven't been on your feet in days. Sit down and let me get Sabrina."

She opened her mouth, but he shook his head. "No arguments." Marrick pushed the button on the bedside stand.

When had he gotten so bossy? But Sam nodded, since she was still wobbly and doubted she would make it across the room anyway.

A minute later, Sabrina showed up. "Well, look who decided to join us."

"I have to go to the trial."

Sabrina narrowed her eyes on Sam. "I'm going to check you over first, and don't even think about fighting me on this."

Sam opened her mouth.

Sabrina shook her head. "Why are doctors and nurses always the worst patients?"

"She almost fell when she stood up," Marrick said.

Tattletale. She scowled up at him.

Sabrina held her hands above Sam's head and closed her eyes. After a few moments she opened them again. "You seem to be stable. You're heading back to normal." She held up her hand before Sam could say anything.

"You need to sit up in bed for a little bit, drink some water, and then we'll get you up and walk you around to make sure you're up for going to the trial."

"I'll be up for it," Sam said.

"I'm sure you will be. I'll be back in a few minutes, and then we'll have you stand up," Sabrina said with a smile.

A smile Marrick did not share when Sam looked at him. He had on his worried face. The face that made her heart flutter.

"I'm okay," she said, squeezing his hand. She realized he hadn't let her hand go since he helped her back up onto the bed. "How's my mom doing?"

"She's okay. She's been under arrest here in the Shamat compound so the clan could watch over her. They've been working on a defense for her, but I haven't been involved with the details."

Sam nodded and took a deep breath. She needed to pull herself together. In hindsight, she had to admit rushing into the trial in her hospital gown wouldn't have gone over well.

She needed to plan through what she was going to do, and from the way Marrick was hovering, she was pretty sure he wouldn't support what she was planning. At all.

But she had to do it. Had to make everything right again if she could. She wasn't the scared little girl anymore, which meant it was time for her to carry some of the responsibility for what had happened.

And she would make this right for her mother. She owed her more than she could ever repay.

"Marrick, can you go to Irina's and get my duffel bag? I want to be able to change into some clean clothes to go to the trial."

Marrick frowned. "*If* you can go to the trial."

She patted his hand. "Right. *If.*"

"I'm worried about you, Sam. You just woke up. What if going to the trial makes you sick again?"

He really was a sweet male.

"I have to be there for my mother. You do understand, don't you? If I feel bad once we get there, I'll tell you."

"Promise?"

"Yes. I'll wait for Sabrina to give me the green light, and then we'll go to the trial."

"Here we go with the lights again," he grumbled.

"You know what I mean."

"I could call Irina and have her bring the bag."

Sam shook her head. "There is no way Irina isn't at the trial."

He sighed.

"Go on, I want to look presentable when I go to the trial." And she needed something from the duffel bag, but she wasn't about to volunteer that tidbit of information.

He nodded and left the room after making her promise she wouldn't leave without him.

Sabrina rejoined her a few minutes later.

"You feeling better?"

"Yes, the room isn't spinning, and I'm thinking clearly."

"Good. Where's Marrick?"

"He went to Irina's to get my duffel bag for a change of clothes."

Sabrina's eyes widened.

"You act like he hasn't left my side or something."

"He hasn't."

"What?"

"He's been in this room with you, without a break, for days."

Her heart started fluttering again.

"Your mom asked him to watch over you."

Her heart slowed down. Honor was Marrick's middle name. Making a promise to her mother would mean he felt the need to keep guard. Wasn't guarding his job, after all?

"Are you going to let me go to the trial?" Sam said, changing the subject.

"Let's get you up and into this chair, and then we'll get you to stand up as soon as we make sure you're not dizzy."

Sabrina supported her as she slid off the bed and sat in the chair. She was feeling fine now. She stood, and Sabrina held her arm for balance until Sam nodded.

Marrick walked back into the room and dropped her duffel on the bed before moving to help support her.

"I'm fine."

"Let's get you changed out of that gown," Sabrina said.

Sam looked at Marrick. "You need to go out into the hall, kind sir."

"She's okay?" he asked Sabrina.

"Yes."

He turned and headed out the door before spinning back around. "If you feel unwell at all, I am bringing you back here, no arguments." And then he was out the door, closing it behind him.

"So bossy," Sam said.

Sabrina chuckled, but Sam couldn't join in the amusement. She was about to do something that would make both Marrick and her mother very angry, but she had no choice.

She needed to make this right.

CHAPTER 30

Marrick was worried about Sam.

Yes, he was ecstatic because she was awake, and her emotions weren't all over the place the way they were when she collapsed. But there was something she wasn't telling him.

She was almost too calm. Why was she so calm? And there was an emotion slowly making its way to the forefront in her psyche. One that scared him more than anything. Determination.

What exactly did she have in mind?

They walked into the meeting hall and sat in chairs at the back.

The room had been reorganized. One table at the front held the Council leaders, and the other table held several Pavel elders. They must be there as judges for the hearing. Then there were seats for the audience members, who were Shamat, Pavel, and the BSR team. To the side sat Gwen, with guards standing on either side of her.

Fortunately, no one turned to look at them, since Boris was in the middle of introducing the Pavel elders.

Sam set her duffel on her lap.

Which was another thing troubling Marrick. Sam had insisted on bringing it to the trial. He wasn't going to argue with her, but he had a fleeting thought that maybe he should have made sure there weren't any weapons in the bag first. Sam loved her mother with a fierceness he'd only seen a few times in his life, and he could only hope she wasn't going to try and do something like rescue her and run away again.

She reached down into the bag and wrapped her hand around something he couldn't see. He tensed. After a moment, she set the bag next to her feet and blew out a breath, and he could actually feel relief float from her.

But her hand was empty, which allowed him to breathe his own relieved sigh.

Boris finished the introductions, and the Pavel elder sitting in the middle of the table read the charges. He finally looked up from the parchment. "Gwendolyn of the Dalmot clan, do you understand the charges against you?"

"I do."

"And what say you on these charges?"

"I'm not guilty. I didn't kill Augustus."

The other elders started murmuring, and he held up a hand, quieting them. "Do you have any evidence to support your claim?"

Marrick turned as Sam's emotions seemed to coalesce into a united front and she stood. "I can support her claim."

Everyone turned toward them.

"Sam!" her mother gasped and tried to stand up, but the guards put their hands on her shoulders and held her in place.

Marrick stood and leaned closer to Sam. "What are you doing?" he murmured.

She continued facing forward as she answered. "Saving my mother."

The elders sputtered, as did the Pavel in the audience.

"Why should we allow you to speak?" one of the elders demanded.

"Because I was with Gus when he was killed."

Everyone started to yell at once. The elder sitting in the middle of the table slammed a gavel down. "Quiet!" He stared at Sam. "Gus?"

"I was too little to be able to say his full name, so he let me call him Gus."

The elder continued. "Why are you just now coming forward with this?"

"I was five years old at the time. I didn't remember what happened until today."

"Isn't that convenient," Akers sneered from his spot at the table.

Sam continued looking at the elder. "It would have been more convenient if I could have remembered years ago so my mother and I didn't have to hide for a crime she didn't commit."

The Pavel started yelling again, and Boris leaped to his feet. "You are guests in my compound, and as such you will calm the hell down or I will throw out everyone who isn't necessary to this trial. Do I make myself clear?"

The Pavel elder nodded. "Boris is right. Everyone sit down so this can be sorted out."

He looked at Sam. "Are you the female who collapsed the other day when your mother turned herself in?"

"Yes. I'm sure that will make it difficult for you to take me seriously, but I ask you to let me speak."

Josiah interrupted. "I have heard enough. This female will do anything to save her mother. The woman who killed my uncle, our leader. They have spent more than a hundred years hiding and lying about who they are. Why would we believe anything these killers and liars have to say?"

The Dalmot leader stood. "Gwen is Dalmot, and she is allowed to have a fair and proper trial. If we don't listen to Sam's testimony, how can we claim to have examined all the evidence?"

"Agreed," the elder said. "Tell us what happened."

Sam cleared her throat and began telling her story. She started with the knock on the door and Gus putting her in the cupboard.

Akers interrupted her again. "How do you know what really happened if you were inside the cupboard the whole time?"

She refused to look at him and instead continued to look at the Pavel elder, who was actually willing to listen to her. "I didn't stay in the cupboard. I crawled out and went to the door of the living room. Gus was on his knees with a demon standing over him holding a knife."

"Did you see the demon's face?"

"Yes." She looked at Akers for the first time and pointed her finger at him. "It was your new leader."

The room erupted, and Marrick jumped in front of Sam, turning into his demon self.

Josiah surged to his feet. "She's lying! She'll do anything to save her mother and her own sorry skin. What better way to instill doubt and cause confusion in our clan than to blame me?" He scowled at Marrick. "You're Pavel, and yet you turn your back on your clan to protect her?"

"Absolutely."

Sam stepped to his side. "I'm telling the truth."

The elder shook his head. "Except you have no proof."

"When Gus was attacked, he said he would make sure the killer would wear the traitor's mark. Do you know what that means?"

The elder's eyes tightened on her. "Yes. Augustus had a ring with a metal crest on the stone that would permanently scar anyone. Centuries ago it was used to mark the guilty so they would bear the consequences of their crime their entire life. Augustus stopped using it that way once he became the leader, but he wore the ring until the day he died."

Sam gasped. "Gus punched his attacker in the chest with the ring, and he drew blood." She turned to Akers. "If you're not guilty, you should be willing to unbutton your shirt and show us your chest."

"I won't show you anything."

"This seems to be a simple, direct way to put a stop to all of this," Boris said.

Akers shook his head, backing away, until a guard stopped him with a hand on his arm.

The elder nodded, and the guard pulled open Akers' shirt, revealing a jagged scar just above his heart.

"It's a scar from a training exercise."

"My, isn't that convenient," Sam said.

Marrick was in awe of this female.

Akers jerked away from the guard. "It doesn't matter whether you believe me or not. We don't have the ring. It's been missing since his death. You can't match it to me."

Sam bent down and pulled a doll out of her duffel, smiling while she dug into the side of the doll and pulled out a ring, holding it up for everyone to see.

Akers snarled and flung his hand up, sending a streak of light through the air toward them. Marrick stepped in front of Sam and grunted when the energy hit his shoulder.

Before Akers could attack again, he flew into the air and then slammed back against the wall.

"You would think he would learn by now," Irina said as she flicked her wrist and he thumped against the wall again.

"Are you okay?" Sam asked Marrick.

He nodded, even though the pain spread from his shoulder into his chest.

Sam walked up to the Pavel elder serving as judge and placed the ring on the table, then went to her mother and hugged her.

Marrick watched them hug as his vision blurred. He heard Sam yelling his name as the pain shot throughout his body and he fell.

Marrick woke up to see Sam asleep in the chair next to his bed. He looked around. Were they back in the same hospital room as before?

He watched her sleep. Her face scrunched up, and he wondered if she was dreaming. He wanted to wake up every morning to that face. After a few minutes she opened her eyes and focused on him.

"I thought I felt someone staring at me. How are you feeling?"

"Fine."

She stood up and looked at the monitors as if she didn't believe him. "You really need to stop getting hurt, you know."

"I think it might be safer for me in the realm."

She frowned. "I'm sorry."

His joke hadn't gone over well. "I was teasing."

"You took a heavy jolt from Akers, but you're going to be fine."

"Where's Akers now?"

"In custody for murder with a side dish of assault for what he did to you."

"And your mother?"

The frown finally disappeared from Sam's face. "They've dropped all charges against her."

"I'm so happy for both of you."

She sighed. "I don't know how to react. I don't remember ever being free to just go somewhere. To hold my head up high and not worry that we might be recognized and arrested."

She blinked shiny eyes. "There are so many things I haven't seen or done. Mom and I used to fantasize about what it would be like to be normal. To travel the world and be front and center instead of hiding."

"Is that what you want to do now? Travel the world with your mother?"

She hesitated. "I haven't had time to think things through, but we can do it now. See the world and decide where we want to call home. We've never had a home before."

"What about here?" he blurted before stopping himself.

"This is an amazing clan. But I don't want to stop Mom from doing all the things she dreamed about for all these years."

His chest felt tight. "That makes sense. You need to be with your mom."

"Yes. I need to be with her right now."

"I understand."

But did he? Because he wanted to tell her she could stay here with him. To let him love her, but she'd never experienced freedom before, much like the realm demons. If his purpose was to free them, how could he cage Sam?

She needed to experience life, and if it meant traveling earth with her mother, then that's what she should do. He wouldn't hold her back.

CHAPTER 31

Sam stood on the balcony of the hotel and looked up at the Eiffel Tower, trying to be excited but failing spectacularly. She could feel her mother's eyes on her, and she pasted on a bright smile before turning to her.

Gwen sighed before going back into the room.

"What's wrong, Mom?"

"What's wrong is, you're just going through the motions. What was the point of this grand adventure, as you called it, if you aren't going to even try to enjoy it?"

Sam followed her into the room. "You're right. I'm sorry."

Gwen stopped. "No. I'm sorry. This is all so new to us. And you still haven't told me what happened when you talked about your feelings with Marrick. I really read that situation wrong."

And that was another thing. The little white lie she'd told her mother was starting to grow horns and eat at her. "Um. I need to tell you something. I didn't exactly talk to Marrick about how I felt."

"Excuse me?"

Oh boy. She had seen that expression before, and it never boded well for her. "I just told him we were finally free, and we needed to find a place to call home."

"And why did you do that?"

Sam hesitated.

"Samantha, you'd better tell me right now what's going on."

"I wanted to be with you. I mean, you've been running for your life, hiding who you are for so long, and now you're free. It's an adjustment."

"Yes. You don't think I can do it on my own?"

Sam sighed. "I didn't want you to be on your own. I wanted you to be able to experience all these wonderful places. How many times did we lie in bed in some seedy motel and talk about all the places we'd go if we were free?"

"And we can do it any time. But not at the expense of your relationship with Marrick."

"I don't know if we have a relationship. We were thrown together. He's so honorable, he felt it was his duty to protect me. When I told him we were going to travel around, he agreed with me."

Gwen shook her head. "You might be correct to a certain extent, but that male has deep feelings for you, Sam. You didn't see what he was willing to do for you. What he did for you when you collapsed."

"What do you mean?"

"He never left your side."

"I know. Sabrina told me. But you made him promise to watch over me."

Gwen closed her eyes for a moment before glaring at her daughter as only a mother could. "Marrick was the one who saved you. Did you know that?"

Sam's heart started thumping in her chest. "No."

"You were paralyzed with emotions and your body shut down. He pulled all those emotions into himself to save you."

"What! He shouldn't have done that. He could have been hurt."

"He was willing to take the risk. If he didn't feel something for you, why would he do that."

Sam shook her head. "I don't know."

"Why are you here with me right now?" Gwen pushed.

Sam threw up her arms. "Because I love you! Because I want to do this for you. All this time, this running and fear and non-life is my fault! If I'd been able to tell someone what happened back then, you wouldn't have had to spend a hundred-plus years on the run."

Her mom grabbed her shoulders. "You were five years old, sweetheart. You saw someone you cared about die. In a bloody, violent way. You are *not* at fault. I'm the one who took you to the healer and had your memories suppressed. If anyone is to blame, it's me. And I am not going to go on a trip around the world with you because you feel guilty. And I'm sure as hell not going to let you throw away a chance at happiness."

"Mom..."

Gwen tilted her head and stared at her.

She was using The Mom Look. The one where she used her X-ray vision to reveal the truth of the matter, and tell you what it was.

"I think this is more than your guilt," she said. "I think you're afraid to admit your real feelings."

Sam sighed. "I don't know what I'm feeling. I've never let myself even dream, much less hope that I could be in a long-term, loving relationship."

Gwen blinked and grabbed Sam's hands. "I'm so sorry. That's on me."

Sam plopped down on the bed. "I think we both need to stop feeling guilty and start living."

"I agree. Dig deep inside. What do you feel when you think of Marrick?"

Warmth swamped Sam, and her eyes burned as tears trickled down her cheeks.

Gwen sat down and wrapped her arm around Sam's shoulder. "That's what I thought. So what do you say we book the next flight back to Cleveland, Ohio, for you?"

Sam turned to face her mother. "What about you?"

"I think I'm going to spend some more time in Paris. Maybe have a fling in the city of love."

Sam tried to school her face, but she must not have succeeded since her mother burst out laughing. "Or maybe I'll just do some sightseeing."

Sam hugged her tight. "I love you, Mom."

"And I love you."

A new thought made her heart thud, and not in a good way. She pushed back and looked at her mom. "What if he doesn't want me now? I walked away from him."

"You're going to need to tell him how you really feel."

Sam swallowed. "And what if it doesn't work?"

"Apologize big time, sweetheart."

———◆◇◆———

Sam crossed the field, looking for signs of smoke. Naya had told her which direction to walk, and she hoped to see the huts soon.

She'd been practicing what she was going to say during her flight back from Paris, and her drive back to the Shamat compound, and her overnight stay at Irina's, who insisted on feeding her and having her rest up after her long flight.

Now, as she got closer to her destination, more and more of the careful speech she'd created on the flight was fleeing her brain. When she finally saw the first puff of smoke, she blew out a nervous breath, but continued forward.

She would not back down now.

And since she was in the middle of another world, turning around wasn't exactly possible anyway. Wasn't that why she decided to come here versus asking him to travel to earth? She needed to make this hard for her. She had some serious making up to do. Like her mom said, "Apologize like you mean it."

Within a couple minutes she reached the outskirts of a small cluster of huts.

Guards turned to face her as she walked toward them.

She hadn't really thought this part through.

What if they tried to stop her? She was pretty sure they weren't used to unscheduled guests in the in-between.

A small murmuring started in the group and a hut door opened and there he was, standing outside his home and staring at her.

His face was an unreadable mask.

She would give anything to have his powers so she could sense what he was feeling. Was he happy to see her, angry? Could he forgive her?

"Hello, Marrick."

"Sam. Why are you here? Has something gone wrong?"

"Everything's fine." She hesitated to say more as the guards crowded around them.

"Can we talk alone?"

"Of course." He gestured toward his hut, and she went inside with him.

His home had a fireplace he used as a cookstove and a small table with two chairs. A door opened into a room with a bed.

"So this is the in-between?" Great, now she was going to babble.

"Yes. What are you doing here?"

"I asked Naya to bring me here."

"Why?"

"Because I want to talk to you, to see you. And tell you how sorry I am for leaving."

"Sam, there's nothing to apologize for. I understand why you feel the need to be with your mother. I don't blame you for leaving. She is your comfort, your home."

Fates, how could he be so understanding? She loved him, and here she was, blowing this.

"I have to apologize because I didn't tell you the truth."

"The truth about what?"

"I didn't tell you how much you mean to me. What I feel for you. I ran away because I was scared."

His eyes widened, and he took a step toward her.

She held up her hand and he stopped.

She needed to get this out or she was going to shatter into a million pieces. "I never hoped to find someone like you. You're honorable, kind, logical, protective, and gorgeous as both a human and a demon."

He smiled then, and her heart started its fluttering again.

"I love you, Marrick. I know it might be too late, but I love you, and I had to tell you. Because *you* are my comfort and my home. I just hope you can forgive me. That it's not too late."

CHAPTER 32

Marrick looked down at the flushed female in front of him. She was so proud, yet courageous enough to be vulnerable. To lay her soul bare for him to accept or reject took a special kind of strength.

Her chin tilted up, but her lip trembled at the same time, and he couldn't wait a second longer to tell her his own truth.

"Sam, I can't forgive you because there's nothing to forgive. You aren't the only one who wasn't forthright. You've been trapped your entire life, unable to experience true freedom, and I didn't want to then ask you to come to the realm and spend years away from your mother and a world you can now truly experience for the first time."

He reached for her hand and wrapped his around it. "I love you, and I want to be with you. But I also feel my purpose is to help make it possible for as many realm demons that want to immigrate to earth to do so. Which means I will be staying here for the foreseeable future. And I didn't want you to have to make a choice."

She rested her hand on his cheek, and he leaned into it slightly.

"Here's the thing, Marrick. I really haven't been able to choose much in my life. Our decisions have been about survival. So to be able to choose something based on love? That's the choice I will make every time."

Before he could respond, she kept talking.

"So if you'll have me, I kind of talked to Sabrina about helping with medical things here in the realm. I can see patients, and order supplies, and train the healers in the clan villages, and be here. She thinks it's a good idea. What do you think?"

He wrapped his arms around her and pulled her against him. What did he think? He thought his heart was going to burst from his chest. Was this truly happening?

He held her back so he could see her face. She was beaming up at him with tears in her eyes, and he couldn't wait anymore.

He leaned down and captured her lips. She melted against him with a soft moan. They tangled together, and he felt whole.

After a few minutes they broke apart to suck air into their lungs.

"So I guess you like the idea?" Sam said with a wicked grin.

Marrick burst out laughing.

Her eyes widened. "I don't know if I have ever heard you laugh like that before. We're going to work on getting you to do a full belly laugh at least once a day."

He picked her up and spun her around.

"I can think of some other things we can practice as well."

"Really?" She nipped his chin. "Can you be a bit more specific?"

"I want to make love to you, explore every inch of this body, starting with your face and neck and moving down from there."

She swallowed. "That's specific, all right."

Marrick carried her to the bedroom and laid her down on the bed. He shed his armor and stood in front of her in his guard uniform.

He turned to his human form.

"You didn't have to turn. I love your demon form too."

His heart thumped while her meaning sank in. She'd been scared of his Pavel form, and knowing her background now, he fully understood why. Knowing she was able to love him and not flinch away was a precious gift.

Marrick lay beside her. The first thing he did was pull the band around her hair away so he could run his fingers through it. It was soft, just as he'd imagined. "I love your hair."

Sam leaned closer and kissed him, and within seconds he was lost. But to be lost in her...

He rolled on top of her and the exploration continued. Soon Sam was squirming beneath him, and as he reached for her shirt, he froze and groaned.

"What's wrong?"

"We can't. With you traveling through the portal and possibly throwing your cycle off, we would need protection to keep you from getting pregnant, and I don't have any."

Sam reached into the back pocket of her pants and pulled out a small box. He looked at her in confusion and her face turned pink. "Uh, I brought some condoms."

He grinned. "You came to the realm with nothing but a box of condoms?"

Her face went from pink to red. "I thought it might be presumptuous to show up with all my things before we had a chance to talk. As for the condoms, just call me optimistic."

Marrick nodded. "I like the name Sam much better."

She laughed. "Stop it! You know what I mean."

"I do. Just so you know, I've never used a condom before."

"Then it's a good thing I'm a nurse. I can train you." She ran her hand up and down his chest. "How do you get this onesie off?"

He pulled the ties apart along his chest and the uniform fell open.

She looked him over. "Wow, you are so much better than the Eiffel Tower."

"What?"

"Just kiss me."

That request he was fully prepared to grant. He caged her under his body and they quickly pulled off their clothes. And between his mouth and hands, he made good on his earlier promise and explored every inch of her.

He loved the breathy sounds she made, and she wasn't shy about telling him what she liked, and *he* liked that.

Then the nurse tutored the demon on the proper use of a condom, spending rather a long time helping him put it on.

He looked down into her eyes and she smiled up at him as they joined. Slow became fast as they moved together. And he absorbed her emotions as if they were his—*or were they his?*—joy, love, pleasure. Abandon.

They crashed over the edge.

They held each other, and his lips rested against her temple as his heart continued to pound a drumbeat. Sam pulled back slightly and then kissed him on the chest, pulling a gasp from him.

"Let me see your amazing demon side."

He turned into his demon.

Then she closed her eyes for a moment and her skin turned a deep blue. When she had finished turning, she opened her now-turquoise eyes and seemed to hold her breath.

Marrick knew the feeling. He could barely breathe himself.

"You are stunning. I am so humbled that you're showing me your demon side. I love you, Sam."

He must have said the right thing because happiness burst from her. Sam kissed his chest and then skimmed her lips over to his nipple, and Marrick was lost again while she tutored him in other wickedly beautiful things.

Later, as he held her against his heart, he knew what he had already suspected. She owned him—heart, body, and soul.

CHAPTER 33

Sam circled her healer students, observing while they wrapped gauze on their "patients." She nodded at some and pointed out a couple of suggestions to others.

"Good job, everyone. Does anyone have any questions?"

They all shook their heads before glancing at each other and snickering. She already knew what they were snickering about, because she felt Marrick come up behind her. She always knew when he was nearby.

Arms wrapped around her middle. "Do you need another patient to practice on?"

The students laughed out loud this time, and she rolled her eyes. "You're too late. We just finished the class."

The students and the clan members who had volunteered to be wrapped up like mummies cleaned up the wrappings and said their goodbyes.

Marrick still held her against him. "Are you ready to head to earth, mate?"

He had been calling her his mate for a while now, but she still got goose bumps when he said it. "Yes. We won't hear the end of it from Irina if we're late for dinner. Do you have any idea what we're celebrating this time?"

"No. You know Irina. She likes to celebrate all sorts of things."

She turned in his arms and kissed him before he let her go, and they left the village and entered a clearing.

Marrick opened the portal and held out his hand to her. They never traveled through the portal without holding hands. After jumping to multiple worlds, Marrick didn't want to risk letting her go.

And she was more than fine with it.

They landed in the Shamat hall meeting room to find Irina and Boris waiting for them.

"Welcome back!" Irina said.

"How are things in the realm?" Boris asked.

"Going well. How are the newest immigrants doing?" Marrick replied.

"Excellent. I think Aleksei and his team have this down to a science now."

"Thanks for inviting us for dinner," Sam said.

Irina smiled. "Of course. Sam, why don't you come with me? Boris can entertain Marrick while we talk."

She looked at Marrick, who responded with a small shrug. "Okay."

They headed out of the community center and went next door to Irina's house, where they walked into a living room full of people.

Naya, Callie, and a very pregnant Lela were there, along with Kyle and Sabrina.

"What's all this?"

"This is your bachelorette-slash-preparation party," Irina said.

"My what!"

"Marrick enlisted us to plan a surprise mating ceremony for the two of you," Naya said.

Sam's mouth fell open before she could stop herself. They had talked about a mating ceremony at some point, but to surprise her...

"I can't read her face. Is that surprised-happy, or surprised-mad?" Kyle asked.

Sam closed her mouth as tears threatened. "Happy. So very happy. I just wish—"

"What do you wish for?" a voice said from behind her.

Sam spun around. "Mom!" She grabbed her in a fierce hug.

"Hi, sweetheart."

"I'm so glad you're here. Are you in on this?"

Gwen smiled. "Of course. Do you honestly think Marrick wouldn't ask my permission to mate you?"

"Of course not."

"And besides, I wouldn't miss this for the world."

Irina rejoined them, carrying a tray of champagne glasses. "Here you both go."

Then she distributed the champagne to the rest of the group. "Lela, the glass with the bow on the stem is sparkling grape juice."

"How was Australia?" Sam asked Gwen.

"Amazing. How is your new job in the realm?"

"Great. I love it. The clans are so welcoming, and I'm teaching healers in all the villages. Plus, I'm there to help in an emergency."

"Not that I need to tell you, but she's great at the job," Sabrina said.

Gwen laid her hand on Sam's shoulder. "I've always been proud of you, but I am so happy knowing you're happy."

"I am. Marrick is wonderful."

"And sexy," Kyle said as everyone cheered and raised their glasses.

"Stop right there. He's like my brother," Naya protested, but she still drank to the toast.

"Hell, everyone is mated or married to somebody's brother in this room," Kyle said.

Everyone laughed and drank to that as well.

Irina herded them into the dining room, where she had set out appetizers. "You all have to eat something. We're not showing up at the ceremony tipsy."

Sam blinked back tears. "I can't believe he did this."

"We're here to help you get ready for your mating ceremony," Kyle said. "Or they are. I'm here for moral support. You don't want me helping with clothes, hair, or makeup."

Sam set down her glass. "What am I going to wear?"

Gwen patted her on the back. "No worries. I've got it covered. Just give me a moment."

She left the room, and Irina wrapped her arm around Sam's shoulders and led her away from the others.

"It's good to have your mother close by."

"Yes."

"I have an idea to keep your mom around for a while. Are you game?"

"Absolutely."

Irina glanced around and lowered her voice. "I'm still working out the details, but I'll let you know more later. Right now we need to get you ready."

She turned Sam around as Gwen emerged from a back room carrying a dress so spectacular that everyone oohed and aahed. Sam blinked and then blinked again. It was a silver-blue color, which was the mating dress color for the Dalmot clan.

"Mom, it's gorgeous."

Gwen beamed. "I'm glad you like it. It's time to start getting you ready."

Sam let the females herd her toward the bedroom.

"Kyle, are you coming?" Sabrina asked.

"Someone's got to eat these appetizers. Irina went to a lot of trouble to make them."

Sam laughed as she sat down on the bed. She was mating Marrick, and her mom and the Shamat clan were going to be a part of it. She was a lucky, lucky female.

———————◆○◆———————

Marrick pulled on his stiff collar again.

"Stop fidgeting," Aleksei said. "I just got your bow tie straight."

"I don't know how you talked me into wearing this tuxedo."

Misha grinned. "Of course you do. Aleksei can talk anyone into anything."

The males standing around him all started to laugh. Misha, Aleksei, and Sergei had helped him get dressed while Misha's BSR teammates, Jean Luc, Jason, and Kyle's mate, Joe, served as ushers and sat the Shamat clan in the chairs overlooking the lake next to the community center. It was a beautiful day, so they had decided to have the ceremony outside.

The twins were bouncing around in front of them asking when they could have some of the mating cake. Misha gazed longingly at the cake before shushing the boys.

"You don't think she's mad, do you?" Marrick asked Aleksei.

"About the surprise mating ceremony?" Aleksei said. "No. If she was, we would have heard about it already from Naya." He tapped his temple. "I told her to let me know if it went south."

Marrick whooshed out a sigh of relief. "Thank the Fates!"

Aleksei slapped him on the back. "I didn't think you had spontaneous in you, but I've never seen you in love before, either."

"True. When you and Naya fell for each other, I thought you were both ridiculous, but I get it now."

Aleksei laughed. "Good to know our ridiculousness finally makes sense."

Boris joined them. "Are you ready?"

"Yes."

They migrated to the front of the chairs, and everyone took their seats, along with Irina and the other females, who had just arrived.

The music began, and Marrick looked down the aisle.

Standing at the end were Sam and her mother.

Gwen held onto Sam's arm and they walked toward him.

Marrick had trouble taking a complete breath.

Sam's hair hung in waves around her shoulders, and she wore a dress that reminded him of moonlight.

She smiled at him, tears in her eyes, and he was lost.

Gwen placed Sam's hand in his and stepped back, taking her seat in the front row.

Marrick and Sam turned to Boris. "I was honored when Marrick asked me to officiate at this mating ceremony. Marrick and Sam have become an important part of this clan and an important part of the immigration. Their selflessness is a gift to us all.

"Before I join them together, I would first offer them membership in this clan. We would be humbled if you became a part of us."

Marrick looked at Sam, who blinked back tears and nodded. Marrick tried to speak, but he had to clear his throat before the words would come. "We would be honored to be members of this clan."

Sam nodded. "What he said."

Everyone chuckled, and Boris rested his hands on their shoulders. "Welcome to the clan. Now let's get this mating ceremony underway."

And in front of their clan—Marrick wasn't sure he would ever get used to it—they were joined as mates.

Now he stood with his arm around his mate, watching their guests, their clan, enjoy the party.

Sam leaned close to him and whispered, "Is it my imagination, or do you think something is going on between my mother and Boris?"

"I think Boris is looking at your mother the way the twins and Misha have been watching our mating cake."

Sam laughed and he loved the sound. Loved—no, adored—*her.*

Naya came to join them with Kara on her hip, and the toddler giggled and batted her eyes at Marrick.

"You are such a flirt. You are going to be the death of your father," Naya said.

"She's never getting mated," Aleksei said as he joined them.

Marrick joined Sam and Naya in their laughter.

A groan had them turning to Lela, who was gripping her stomach with Sergei helping her stay on her feet.

Sabrina rushed over to them and spoke to Lela in low tones.

Sam tensed next to him.

"I think it's baby time," Sabrina said to the group.

"Can we just once have a mating ceremony without a baby being born?" Kyle exclaimed as her mate, Joe, wrapped his arm around her shoulder.

"At least I don't have to deliver the baby this time," Misha said.

"Sorry for the interruption. Everyone stay and enjoy yourselves," Lela insisted before moaning again.

Sergei picked Lela up, and Sabrina walked alongside them all the way to the hospital.

Sam was practically bouncing on her feet next to him.

"Go on, mate. I know you can't stand back and not help."

She looked up at him. "Are you sure?"

He nodded and Sam stood on her toes and kissed him before picking up her skirts, kicking off her shoes, and running across the grass toward the hospital.

The group laughed as they watched his barefoot mate streak across the lawn in a mating dress.

Gwen tucked her arm through Marrick's. "That's our girl."

"Yes. And we're so blessed."

Gwen pulled on his arm, and he leaned down. She kissed him on the cheek before whispering in his ear. "We are, but I think Sam is blessed to have you as well. Thank you."

He blinked back tears as he thanked the Fates for his new mate and clan.

Hours later, Sam cuddled in his arms as they settled down for the night.

"What a day," Sam said.

Marrick laughed. "That's an understatement, as you earthers would say."

"It's a good thing we got Lela to the hospital when we did. She had that baby really fast. And he's a big boy."

"A new addition to the clan."

"He's not the only one. I can't believe we're members of the Shamat clan."

"Yes. That was a surprise," Marrick said.

Sam sat up and turned to him. "But it wasn't the only, or even the best, surprise today. You planned a surprise mating ceremony. You are in so much trouble."

He nuzzled her neck. "Really?"

She leaned her head to the side to give him more access.

"No. I loved it. I'm so glad Mom was there."

"I wouldn't have had it without her."

"And that's one of the reasons why I love you," Sam said as she kissed along his jaw.

"One of the reasons?"

"Yes." She pushed him onto his back and straddled him. "Let me tell you the other reasons." She kissed him on the chest, and he bit back a groan.

"I'm willing to listen."

She chuckled, low and sexy, before proceeding to tell *and* show how much she loved him.

And Marrick's heart was finally, truly full.

THANKS!

Thank you for taking the time to read *Demons In The Rough*. The next book in this series is *Demons Just Want To Have Fun*. It's the final book in the Realm series and it is all about Boris! How can I not give Father Bear his own happy ever after?

I hope you enjoyed Marrick and Sam's story. Please consider telling your friends about it or posting a short review. Word of mouth is an author's best friend, and much appreciated. Thank you! – AE

If you would like to know when my next books will be released, please check out my website aejonesauthor.com

Please turn the page to find a list of my other books.

Other Books By AE

Mind Sweeper Series
Mind Sweeper
The Fledgling
Shifter Wars
The Pursuit
Sentinel Lost

The Realm Series (Mind Sweeper Spin Off)
Demons Will Be Demons
Demons Are A Girl's Best Friend
Demons Are Forever
Demons In The Rough
Demons Just Want To Have Fun

The Pack Series (Mind Sweeper Spin Off)
Shifter and the Succubus

Paranormal Wedding Planner Series
In Sickness and In Elf
From This Fae Forward
To Have and To Howl
For Better or For Wolf
For Witch or For Poorer
Till Demon Do Us Part

The Sentries Series
Dragon Kissed
Dragon Charmed

ACKNOWLEDGMENTS

Thanks to Sandra Owens an amazing writer who also reads for me and lets me know when I'm heading down the wrong path. Thanks for speaking up about this book and helping me turn one story into two!

Thanks to my amazing editors, Faith Freewoman and Lea Schafer for making this story sparkle.

And thanks to Melissa for creating an awesome cover for Marrick's book!

ABOUT THE AUTHOR

Growing up a TV junkie, AE Jones oftentimes rewrote endings of episodes in her head when she didn't like the outcome. She immersed herself in sci-fi and soap operas. But when *Buffy* hit the little screen, she knew her true love was paranormal. Now she spends her nights weaving stories about all variations of supernatural—their angst and their humor. After all, life is about both...whether you sport fangs or not.

AE won the prestigious Golden Heart® Award for her paranormal manuscript, Mind Sweeper, which also was a RITA® finalist for both First Book and Paranormal Romance. AE is also a recipient of the Booksellers' Best Award and is a National Readers' Choice Award Finalist, Holt Award of Merit Finalist and a Daphne du Maurier Finalist.

AE lives in Ohio surrounded by her eclectic family and friends who in no way resemble any characters in her books. *Honest.* Now her two cats are another story altogether.

Learn more about AE and her books on her website aejonesauthor.com